Childish
SPIRITS

To Mia and Emily

Best Wishes
   Rob Keeley

By the same author

The Alien in the Garage and Other Stories
The (Fairly) Magic Show and Other Stories
The Dinner Club and Other Stories

Childish
SPIRITS
ROB KEELEY

Matador
9 Priory Business Park,
Wistow Road, Kibworth Beauchamp,
Leicestershire. LE8 0RX
Tel: (+44) 116 279 2299
Fax: (+44) 116 279 2277
Email: books@troubador.co.uk
Web: www.troubador.co.uk/matador

ISBN 978 1783064 618

British Library Cataloguing in Publication Data.
A catalogue record for this book is available from the British Library.

Typeset in Book Antiqua by Troubador Publishing Ltd, Leicester, UK

Matador is an imprint of Troubador Publishing Ltd

Printed and bound in the UK by TJ International, Padstow, Cornwall

Chapter One

Charlie slammed the boot of the car. He was holding an enormous holdall, which he flung onto an ever-growing pile of luggage that lay on the gravel.

"Two shops," he said. "Two shops, one of which sells hats."

His younger sister Ellie emerged from the rear passenger seat.

"What?"

"Two shops," Charlie said. "One pub. Called the Jolly Ferret – I mean, who thinks these things up?"

"What are you on about?" Ellie asked.

"This place." Charlie pulled up the hood of his top. "Two shops. One pub. A church."

"Have you seen my portfolio?" Ellie poked about among the pile of luggage.

There was a crash as a plastic laundry basket that Charlie had balanced on top of the pile collapsed sideways onto a box of groceries.

Charlie ignored the mess.

"Two shops," he said, "one pub. A church. A village store. Two people riding moth-eaten horses, and a maypole." He shuddered. "Welcome to our new home."

Ellie walked around the car and opened the rear

door on the opposite side.

"Here it is." She lifted out the concertina-like folder that contained her most recent work. "Hey, give me a hand with my easel, will you?"

Charlie rolled his eyes.

"Why couldn't I have been an only child? There you go." He lifted the wooden easel from the back seat, shoving it down in front of Ellie. "So that's what's been digging into me since Watford."

Ellie wasn't listening. She turned to look up at Inchwood Manor.

The house was huge, and white, and lined with timber frames. Tall chestnut trees surrounded, reaching out towards the upper floors. A stone archway framed the open front doors. Written above were some words in a language Ellie couldn't understand. *Veritas… vos…*

Charlie was looking at the Manor like a prisoner being shown his cell.

"I can just see us, in a year's time," he said. "You up there, painting the Mona Lisa. Me, trying to make a fire to keep out the cold in this dump."

"We'll be OK," Ellie said. "Mum says our flat's got central heating."

Charlie ignored her.

"I read up about this place," Ellie went on. "It's been here over five hundred years."

Charlie grimaced.

"Bet the bogs have too."

"It's got a priest's hole," Ellie said. "And a hidden chamber in the library."

2

Charlie smirked.

"I suppose there's a gang of diamond thieves hiding there?"

The smirk disappeared from his face as he tried to lift Ellie's suitcase out of the back of the car.

"Oi! Miniature one! Why am I doing all the work?"

There was another crash.

"Hey, careful!" Ellie ran back. "Those are my oil paints!"

There was a crunching of gravel as three adults stepped out of the house.

The first was Ellie and Charlie's Mum. The second was a plump young man in a pinstriped suit that was slightly too tight for him.

Last to come was an elderly lady in tweeds. She was carrying a small suitcase, which she set down upon the gravel.

Mum viewed the family chaos beside the car.

"These are my children. Charlie… and Ellie. This is Marcus, our Site Manager from Journeyback UK."

"Chas," said Charlie. He moved in front of Ellie to shake hands with Marcus. "Hi."

"And this," said Mum, "is Miss Harvey. Who has very kindly given us the job of looking after Inchwood."

Ellie shook hands.

For a second, the sunlight caught Miss Harvey's brooch. It was oval, with a three-dimensional picture – a strange, swirling design…

A car horn sounded. Ellie turned to see a minicab waiting across the courtyard.

Miss Harvey turned to Marcus.

"Well. I wish you every success." She frowned. "Make sure you look after the place. My family has been here for over a hundred years. I don't want Journeyback turning it into some kind of theme park."

"Don't worry, Miss H," Marcus said. He failed to notice her wince. "That's what we do. Journeyback UK."

"Where the past –" Charlie spoke up, "– is now!"

Marcus looked impressed.

"Someone's done their homework."

"And I shall be popping back," Miss Harvey said, "to make sure everything is in order." Her voice softened a little. "Remember, I'll only be down in the village, if you have any queries."

"I'm sure we'll be calling on you quite a bit," Mum said.

Ellie's attention had wandered. Stepping away from the group, she stood looking up at the house.

She stared at a window on the first floor.

She blinked.

There was a face there. Someone was watching her.

It looked like… Ellie squinted to see.

It was the face of a boy.

Of about her own age.

She was distracted by the scattering of gravel as Miss Harvey's taxi drove away.

"And now," said Mum to Marcus, as they waved her off, "it's over to us."

"Mum?" Ellie ran up to her mother. "I thought you said we were on our own here?"

Mum smiled, puzzled.

"We are."

"'Til all the visitors start flocking in," said Marcus. "And that's what your wonderful Mum is gonna help us with."

Mum smiled modestly.

"Then –" Ellie pointed to the window. "Who's that up there?"

"Where?" Mum turned and looked up. The others did the same.

The window was empty.

"Must have been a trick of the light," Mum said. "It's the glass they used in these old windows."

"And that reminds me," Marcus said. "The first thing you and me need to do, Judith, is look over this place from top to bottom. There's woodworm, damp, so much dust we'd have every asthmatic suing us. I don't know how the old bat lived in the place."

"Better get started, then," Mum said.

She headed after Marcus, calling instructions back to Ellie and Charlie.

"Just bring the essential stuff in to start with! We can unload properly later…"

Charlie turned back to the mountain of luggage. His face said it all.

Ellie remained where she was, staring up at the empty window.

Chapter Two

Ellie and Charlie entered the cold and draughty hallway. Charlie still had his hood up, as if to protect himself from his surroundings.

He sniffed.

"What a dump."

"I love it." Ellie was scuttling along, drinking in the dark oak panelling, the black-and-white checked floor tiles, the portraits, the worn chairs, the ferns in a bowl on the hall table… "Can't you just *feel* history all around you?"

Charlie sniffed. "I can smell it, all right."

"It's going to be fun," Ellie went on. "I can write here, and paint. The estate's massive. There's a lake, and an island with a stone folly. Maybe we can have a picnic there!"

Charlie rolled his eyes.

Ellie moved faster, catching up with the adults. Mum and Marcus were talking.

"We've already got most of the staff organised," Marcus was saying. "Wardens, cleaners, maintenance. That kind of thing. But what we really need is to make this place happen."

He quickened his pace.

"I'm thinking…fun days, actors doing the historical bit, concerts on the lawns later in the summer…"

He smirked at Mum.

"And for that, we need you. 'Soon as I mentioned Events Organiser, everyone told me: Judith's your woman."

"I've been in the commercial sector two years." Mum smiled. "I think my good works might be a little rusty."

Marcus wasn't listening.

"Then," he went on, "after that… who knows? Weddings, conferences… I'm not just in this for old biddies buying tea towels. Inchwood Manor is going places. And you, Judith, are coming too."

Ellie followed the adults up a vast staircase.

"I'll give you the tour," Marcus said. "Then after that I'll take you to your flat."

"Fine," Mum said.

"I've set up the Site Office on this floor," Marcus continued. "Used to be the housekeeper's room. Right in the centre of things, but still away from prying eyes…"

He reached the top of the stairs a second ahead of Mum and Ellie. A slouching Charlie brought up the rear.

The corridor in which they found themselves had the same red carpet as the staircase. There was more panelling, and there were paintings, with a suit of armour standing guard.

"You could have had rooms up here," Marcus said, "but we do have to think of the winter time. It's gonna get *way* colder than this."

Ellie grinned as she saw Charlie's face.

As the others moved off along the corridor, she paused to look at an oil painting on the wall.

A sound reached her ears.

Nearby, someone was whistling.

Ellie turned.

It was coming from behind a door at the end of the corridor.

She realised that this door must lead to the room she had viewed from outside. The room with that window.

Ellie hesitated a moment. Then she approached the door.

"Hello?"

There was silence suddenly.

Ellie cleared her throat.

"Anyone in there?"

There was no answer.

Slowly, Ellie reached out, turned the handle and pushed open the door.

Her eyes widened.

She found herself in a children's nursery that looked as if it hadn't been disturbed for decades. Dust-covered toys lay everywhere… a rocking horse with a mane of real horsehair … several ranks of brightly-painted tin soldiers parading on a shelf… a magnificent clockwork train set laid out on a large table.

Bookshelves lined the whole of one wall. She read some of the titles. *Alice's Adventures in Wonderland.*

Gulliver's Travels. The Boy's Book of Railways.

In the window, framed by faded pink curtains, stood a piano. It looked dirty and disused, like everything else in the room, yet its lid lay open, ready for someone to play.

Ellie paused.

"Anybody here?"

She took a few more steps into the room.

"Hello?"

Slowly, she advanced towards the window. Slowly, she reached out a hand towards the piano…

"BOO!"

Ellie jumped.

She turned.

Charlie stood there, grinning.

"Charlie!" Ellie aimed a swipe at him. He dodged, effortlessly.

"Mum and Marcus were looking for you," Charlie said. "You shouldn't have wandered off. Hey, you'll be all right in here."

He picked up a piece of the train set, a white-painted model of a signal box.

"Somewhere for the little children to play."

"Hey, leave it, Charlie!" Ellie took the signal box and returned it to its place in the layout. "That's not ours, you'll get us in trouble."

She turned away and headed back to the window. There was a wonderful view from there. They seemed to be incredibly high up, and she almost felt she could reach out and touch the tops of the old chestnut trees.

She could see hills and fields beyond.

It was weird. To think that, once, all this had belonged to just one family…

She winced, as a horrible, jarring note came from the piano behind her. She turned to see Charlie idly pressing keys.

"*Stop* it, Charlie!"

"Just thought you might want to add composing to your many talents." Charlie pressed a couple more keys randomly. "Don't suppose this has been used much since Beethoven slung it out –"

There was a crashing of chords, as the piano lid slammed down.

"Aaagh!" Charlie clutched his hand. He glared at Ellie. "You did that deliberately!"

"I never touched it!" Ellie yelled.

"Well, someone did." Charlie felt his fingers tenderly. "Ow."

"Serves you right," Ellie told him.

Charlie headed for the corridor, still rubbing his hand.

"Didn't want to come here, anyway. Sooner we go back to London, the better."

He slammed the door.

Ellie stood for a moment, staring around the empty room, at the piano, the dusty toys, the faded spines of the books.

She was on her own again. Yet somehow she felt that someone else was in there with her.

Chapter Three

"Marcus brought you up here for a tour of the place." Mum was looking annoyed as Ellie came out of the nursery. "Not to go wandering off."

"That's OK, Judith." Marcus paused. "All the same, you want to be careful. There's places up here, not had their Health and Safety clearance yet."

Charlie rubbed his hand.

"So I noticed."

"Anyway…" Marcus headed for the staircase. "I'll take you down again now. Show you your own place. Miss Harvey's old flat."

He moved off.

Ellie hesitated by the nursery door.

She could hear the whistling again.

She reached out towards the door handle.

"Ellie!" Mum called, from halfway down the stairs. "Come *on!*"

Reluctantly, Ellie obeyed.

"You have got to be joking."

Marcus had led them to the far end of the hall and through a green baize door that looked like a snooker table on hinges.

They found themselves in a large, white-painted room, with a wide fireplace and small, high windows. There was very little light, and not much furniture. A battered old sofa faced an even more battered portable TV. There was a plastic-topped kitchen table, and various chairs that didn't match either the table or each other. There was a stained and dirty sink and an ancient and grubby fridge.

"*This* is our flat?" Charlie asked. "So this is what – the kitchen?"

"And the dining room." Mum grinned. "And the lounge. It was the servants' hall, back in the day. Miss Harvey has arthritis, she couldn't manage the stairs, so –"

"We've come all the way from London." Charlie blinked. "To a mansion, this size. And we're living in *one room*?"

"Yeah, well…" Marcus shuffled. "I'll leave you to settle in."

He turned to Mum.

"Touch base first thing tomorrow, Judith. We need to start devising a business cycle for the Phase One Events Schedule."

He made his exit quickly.

Charlie glanced around. "This gets worse."

"Right," said Mum. "Sleeping accommodation. Ellie – I think your room's through here."

She opened a door to a small room which contained a camp bed and very little else.

"It's the old scullery. We're lucky, actually. Most old houses, these rooms would be below stairs."

She moved back to the centre of the main room.

"Charlie – you're sleeping in here."

"So where's *my* bed, then?" Charlie sank onto the sofa.

The grin returned to Mum's face.

"You're sitting on it. It's a sofa bed. Oh, come on, Charlie, you know how to set them up…"

Charlie rolled his eyes. He stood up and started trying to find his bed beneath the cushions.

"Ellie –" Mum paused. "Where are you?"

"In my room!" Ellie's cheery voice came from beyond the scullery door. "I think this flat's going to be cool."

The usual chaos of moving in followed. There were holdalls to unpack… groceries to unload… Ellie's paints fought Mum's folders and Charlie's toiletries in a battle for supremacy.

By nine p.m., they had settled in as best they could. The remains of a takeaway lay on the table, where Mum sat studying paperwork. Ellie sat beside her, scribing away on scrappy pieces of notepaper. Charlie was struggling to keep a picture on the portable TV as he tried to watch his reality shows. On the flickering screen, which Charlie was viewing intently, a young man in a new suit was standing in front of a grim-faced panel of businesspeople, trying to sell his idea for a floating bistro.

Mum yawned.

"I think that's enough Phase One for one night."

She pushed her papers aside, turning her attention to Ellie. "What are you working on?"

Ellie shrugged.

"Just a few ideas for poems."

"Can I see?" Mum picked up the top sheet of paper and read the title. "*The Nursery*. Is this based on that room upstairs?"

"Could be." Ellie politely took the sheet of paper back.

"You should be able to find a lot of inspiration here," Mum said.

Ellie took up her mobile, finishing off a text message.

"Who are you texting?" Mum asked.

"Dad," said Ellie. "Let him know we've arrived OK." She paused. "Well, no one else called him, did they?"

"I'll be calling him," Mum said.

She softened her tone.

"Ellie, I know this has been a bit of an upheaval for you and Charlie. Leaving London. Changing schools…"

"It's cool," said Ellie.

"It's not forever, you know. I'm only on a twelve-month contract. And we can go back on visits. You'll still see your Dad…"

"I've told you." Ellie sent the text.

She sat looking at the mobile phone.

"It's cool."

Three hours later, the flat lay in darkness.

Charlie was asleep on the sofa bed. Mum was sleeping on the opposite side of the servants' hall from Ellie, in what had once been the larder.

Ellie lay awake in her tiny bedroom. She couldn't sleep. The excitement of the day, mingling with the mystery of the room upstairs, had left her brain too active.

There was a large clock on the wall just outside Ellie's door.

Tick. Tick. Tick…

"Shut up…" Ellie muttered.

She reached out of bed, found her watch. Eleven fifty-seven. There were hours to go until morning.

She lay down again and closed her eyes.

She remembered what Dad used to say to her, when she was little and couldn't sleep.

"*Think nice thoughts…*"

Ellie tried to imagine living at Inchwood in the old days. Going out for a walk, maybe, amidst the chestnut trees, first thing in the morning, while all was still. Then back to the house for breakfast, with servants to make it. Painting at the high upper windows… playing in the nursery upstairs…

Somewhere very near, a door slammed against a wall.

Ellie sat bolt upright in bed.

Ellie crept out of her room.

The flat was quiet and still. Only the clock ticking broke the silence of the night.

Ellie stared.

The main door into the flat was wide open.

It had definitely been shut when they'd gone to bed. It couldn't just be the draught. The first thing Mum had worked out was how to lock the door.

Ellie crept past Charlie. He muttered in his sleep, stirred slightly.

Tick. Tick. Tick –

Silence.

Ellie blinked.

The clock had stopped.

It was midnight.

Ellie froze. She could hear a faint melody.

The whistling had started again.

And this time, it was here in their flat.

Ellie stood, listening. The sound was moving across the room.

The main door slammed shut.

Charlie shifted uncomfortably.

After a moment, Ellie breathed.

She stood wondering what to do. Go back to bed? That made sense. The flat was cold, and bed, if not warm, had at least been warmer. The house was dark. And she would be alone.

But outside, a short walk away, lay the nursery – and the answer to who was whistling that tune…

Ellie grabbed her fleece from a nearby chair. She put it on over her night things, zipped it right up to the neck. She grabbed Charlie's torch from the floor by the sofa bed.

Then she headed for the door.

With only the torch to light her way, Ellie emerged into the hall.

She shivered slightly, as she heard whistling – just a few notes.

She jumped, as she heard another door slam. She used the torch to find it. Nearby, a narrow wooden door was blowing in the cold night air. Beyond it was a flight of steep, stone steps, leading downward. A cellar, she supposed. She pulled the door shut.

There was silence.

Then, Ellie heard another sound. Footsteps on the staircase to the first floor.

She grasped the banister rail, and crept upstairs.

She reached the upper corridor just in time to hear the slamming of another door. Somehow, she knew which door that would be.

She moved cautiously towards the nursery.

She paused. She could hear the melody again. But this time, it wasn't being whistled.

Someone was playing the piano.

Ellie opened the door.

Silence.

Ellie stood in the doorway and stared. A shaft of moonlight illuminated the scene. The nursery was empty. The soldiers looked blankly back at her. The rocking horse seemed to be smiling.

Leaving the door slightly ajar, Ellie crossed to the piano. She had left the lid down. But now it was raised again.

She turned.

Her eyes grew.

The train set had come to life. The key was turning itself in the side of the engine.

The train started to move around the track.

"Hello?" Ellie had summoned all her courage to speak the word, yet it came out in a tiny whisper. She cleared her throat. "Hey, who is that?"

She forced herself to raise her voice as she moved forward.

"I'm not frightened, you know. So you can forget that, right from the start."

She took another step towards the moving train.

Then another…

"BOO!"

Ellie froze. Then she relaxed.

And she'd thought he was asleep.

"Charlie!" Ellie snorted. "Honestly, you're so pathetic. Did you really think you'd get me again –?" She turned.

And the torch fell from her fingers, rolling across the nursery floor.

Standing before her was a boy.

But it wasn't Charlie.

It was a boy the same age as her. He had very thick blond hair, bright blue eyes and a grin that made her feel she was about to become the victim of a particularly nasty practical joke.

She could see him quite plainly.

But she could also see *through* him. She could see the train set, and the bookshelf beyond.

And in that moment, Ellie knew that this was no ordinary boy.

Chapter Four

For a moment, Ellie simply stood.

The boy also stood still, grinning, watching her. Enjoying her fear.

Ellie stared at him. He was dressed like no other boy she had ever seen before – a tweed suit complete with waistcoat, a smart shirt and a tie that was slightly crooked. Everything was beautifully tailored.

Whoever he was, his Mum and Dad must have been rich.

This was *his* place, she could tell that. He fitted in perfectly with his surroundings, the train set and toys and books. Everything here was his.

And Ellie had an uncomfortable feeling that she was butting in.

"Oh."

Ellie jumped as the boy spoke.

"I'm awfully sorry." The boy's voice was mocking, and incredibly upper-class. "Did I scare you?"

He closed his grin into a smirk.

"Serves you right. Barging into a fellow's house uninvited –"

Ellie opened her mouth to reply.

"– and don't tell me your mother's come to work here," the boy went on. "Because this house – is *mine*.

And *I* say who comes to work here."

His blue eyes gleamed.

"Are you frightened of me?"

Ellie swallowed.

"No."

"Why not?"

"Because…" Ellie caught her breath. "Because… you're not real. You're a ghost."

"How do you know?"

"What?" Ellie blinked.

"How do you know I'm not real?" the boy asked. "Maybe *I'm* the real one. Maybe *you're* the one who's just pretend."

He smiled.

"Or are you right after all? Maybe it *is* a ghost standing in front of you – or behind you!"

Ellie spun around.

All of a sudden, the boy was standing behind her. He gave her another smirk.

"Look…" Ellie tried to steady her voice. "You're not scaring me –"

"Or maybe," the boy continued, "you're not seeing me at all. Maybe you're still asleep. Maybe I'm a dream. A figment of your imagination."

He took a step forward.

"Now you see me –"

He disappeared.

There was silence.

Ellie took a deep breath. She looked left – right – no sign of him…

Then she gave another yell as the posh little voice came from nowhere.

"And now you don't!" the voice called. "But I'm jolly well still here, so there! See?"

Ellie trembled as she saw her own hair rise into the air, lifted by an unseen hand. She shouted as she felt the invisible boy give it a tug.

"Ow! That hurt, you little –"

The boy reappeared, narrowing his eyes at her.

"Still think I'm not real?"

The next moment, he was gone again.

"Now where am I? Can you guess, Little Miss Eleanor? Oh yes, I was downstairs earlier. You didn't see me, but I was there all right. And by-the-by, I read your poetry. It's rotten!"

Ellie yelled as she felt someone stamp on her foot.

The boy reappeared, smiling sweetly.

Boiling over, Ellie grabbed a thatched cottage from the train set and hurled it at him.

Before it could reach its target, the boy disappeared, reappearing on the other side of the room.

"Oh, bad luck!" He smiled at Ellie. "You know, you've got a lot of nerve. For a girl."

Ellie grabbed another item from the layout – a green-painted water tower – and gave it her best throw.

The boy repeated the trick, returning to his previous place.

"Maybe you'd like to be my companion! I get so lonely up here, all alone."

In less than a second, he disappeared and reappeared behind Ellie.

"Boo!"

Ellie staggered forward.

She turned, yet again, to face him.

"We could play up here!" the boy went on. "You could join in all my games! *If* you do just what you're told. Or maybe…"

His voice hardened.

"Maybe it would be more fun… *just to keep you in the dark.*"

The next moment, Ellie found her feet leaving the floor.

Something like a tornado hit her. The nursery door shot open, and Ellie found herself flying backwards, propelled by an invisible force into the darkness beyond.

"Good night!"

At breakneck speed, Ellie flew back along the corridor –

Down the stairs –

And, without even seeing their flat –

THUMP!

She found herself back on her bed.

Ellie lay there for a moment, gasping.

Out of the darkness came the faint sound of the boy's mocking laughter.

Chapter Five

"Charlie…?" Ellie said.

She and Charlie were at breakfast. She had a bowl of cereal in front of her, which she was ignoring.

She tried not to look repulsed at the sight of her elder brother stuffing down toast and lime marmalade.

"What?" Charlie asked, with his mouth full.

Ellie hid her disgust.

"Have you ever seen something, which you knew you'd seen. But which you couldn't have seen –"

Charlie sniggered.

"Didn't you get any sleep last night either?"

"*You* did," Ellie told him. "You were fast asleep, when I –"

Charlie frowned.

"When you what?"

"Nothing." Ellie fell silent.

"Oh, come on, you two!" Mum bustled into the room, seizing papers and files, shoving them all into her briefcase. She grabbed an official-looking badge and hung it on its ribbon around her neck. On it was the Journeyback logo. "It's not a holiday, this, you know. It's a working day. I've got to go through our whole strategy with Marcus this morning."

"I might come and give you a hand," said Charlie. "Show you how the *young* entrepreneurs do it."

Mum pulled a face.

"Just for that, you can do all the data entry."

"And what about *her*?"

"I was hoping you might help with the creative side, Ellie," Mum said. "I've seen the draft of the children's guidebook for this place and it looks as if it was written by a four-year-old."

"There you are," Charlie said. "Just your age group."

Ellie stuck her tongue out at him.

"Perhaps you could give it the once-over," Mum continued. "Maybe do some research on the Internet. Rewrite it into something kids might actually want to read."

"Yeah, OK." Ellie was looking thoughtful. "I'd like to find out some more about this place."

"Right." Mum produced her laptop from its bag. "You can use this. Guidebook's on the desktop."

She headed for the green baize door.

"Come on, Charlie, let's go and see if they've got me a desk up there yet."

Charlie closed the door.

Ellie rose and took her breakfast dishes over to the sink. Mum's task could be the perfect opportunity for her to find some answers.

She turned on the tap. Nothing happened.

Ellie twisted it first one way, then the other.

The next moment, without a touch from her, the tap was suddenly full on.

Drenched, Ellie yelled. She pushed at the tap, but it refused to budge.

She heard a sound familiar from the previous night. A faint, childish laughter.

"All right!" Ellie shouted. "I know it's you! Wherever you are, come out!"

The boy appeared, resplendent in his tweed suit, and casually snapped his fingers. The tap turned itself off.

"Do you like our servants' hall?" he asked. "Used to be so much nicer. I often came down here to be charming to the staff. Especially at mealtimes. Do you know, they all used to stand up when I came in? Mrs Roberts the cook thought I was sweet, she'd give me gingerbreads and meringues. Nice old trout. Do you like gingerbread –?"

"WHO ARE YOU?" Ellie bellowed. "And what are you doing in our flat?"

"Oh, I'll be everywhere," the boy said. "As long as you're in my house. I can hide anywhere I choose."

He vanished. But Ellie could still hear him.

"I could be here!"

Ellie blinked as cupboard doors opened and slammed.

"There!"

Ellie gave a cry of rage as her poems flew up from the table, twisted and crumpled in mid-air and fell to the floor.

Then – silence.

Slowly, Ellie picked up a tea towel, to dry herself.

She looked around. There was no sign of her visitor.

To calm her nerves, she lifted her lukewarm cup of tea to her lips.

"And everywhere!"

The boy's face grinned at her out of the mug.

Ellie shrieked and spilt the tea.

A moment later, the boy reappeared in the room, looking gleeful.

"Good job it was going cold, eh?"

He disappeared again.

Cautiously, Ellie stepped across the room, looking at every object where he might be hiding.

Not the mug again… not Mum's laptop carrier…

Then she looked at her own small shoulder bag.

"I say!" A cheerful voice came from inside the bag. "What a lovely lot of things you've got in here!"

But this time, Ellie was ready for him. With one swift movement, she grabbed the bag and slammed it down onto the tabletop, holding onto it hard.

"Right! Got you!"

"Aargh!" the boy's voice yelled. For the first time, he sounded unsure of himself. "Let me go!"

"Not until you've answered a few questions!" Ellie shouted.

"You're suffocating me!" the voice howled.

"How can I suffocate you?" Ellie held the bag firmly. "You're a ghost!"

"I'm warning you –" the voice went on.

"I want to know who you are!" Ellie told the bag.

"Let me go this instant!" the boy's voice cried. "I'm

not without influence, you know!"

From the table, the squeezy bottle of tomato ketchup rose into the air. A carton of milk emerged from the fridge to join it.

"Now," the voice came. "Are you going to let me go?"

"No!"

A jet of ketchup caught Ellie right between the eyes. The carton opened itself and began to add milk to the water that still covered her neck and shoulders.

"Let me go!" the bag screamed.

Ellie held it tightly.

"Not until you tell me who you are, and what this is all about!"

She looked up.

Mum and Charlie were standing there.

She looked at the ketchup bottle and milk carton.

They had dropped harmlessly to the floor.

"Ellie!" Mum stared in disbelief. "What in the name of –?"

"Told you she was acting weird," Charlie said. "Must be this place."

Mum's face was stern.

"I'm waiting, Ellie."

Ellie stood in silence.

Mum grabbed a dishcloth from the sink and flung it at Ellie.

"I know coming here has been difficult for you. But I thought you were more mature than to react in this silly way."

She pointed to the battle zone.

"You can start by clearing all this up, right now. Then you can finish the rest of the unpacking. I don't want you to do the guidebook any more. I'll give it to someone who can be trusted."

She grabbed a plastic bag of folders from next to the TV set and strode out, followed by a grinning Charlie.

Slowly, Ellie opened her shoulder bag, which she had released when Mum appeared. She took a look inside.

It was clear there was no one in.

Invisibly, the boy blew a perfect raspberry.

Chapter Six

"Inchwood Manor was gifted to Sir Henry Fitzberranger by the Crown," the schoolmarmish Internet voice informed Ellie, "in fifteen hundred and eighty-six. It remained in the Fitzberranger family until nineteen hundred and ten, when, with no surviving male heir, the estate passed to the only surviving child, Sarah, and her husband Mortimer Harvey."

"Miss Harvey's family…" Ellie muttered.

Slowly, she raised her eyes from the computer, looking upward in the direction of the nursery.

"No surviving male heir…"

She clicked at the mouse.

"Well, come on, then! Tell me his name! How old was he?"

Her eyes widened as she looked at the screen.

"Edward…"

The next moment, three things happened at once.

The screen went blank. The light above her went out. And beneath her feet, Ellie felt a tremor.

She looked down. The floor was starting to shake.

She leapt to her feet.

"Edward!"

She ran for the door.

Ellie dashed out of the flat and into the hall. The tremors were getting worse. A portrait fell to the floor as she moved towards the staircase.

Halfway up the stairs, she almost cannoned into Mum on her way down.

"Ellie!"

"Mum? What's happening?"

"I think it's some kind of seismic disturbance. Now, listen. We need to get out of the house."

"Earthquake!" Charlie charged past them. For the second time, Mum was nearly knocked flying.

"Charlie…"

"Judith!" Marcus's voice came from below.

Mum hurried on downstairs.

Ignoring Mum's instructions, Ellie headed for the nursery.

"Edward?" Ellie flung open the nursery door.

All around her, the toys were taking on lives of their own, shuddering, moving. The train moved forward along the track. Juddered and stopped. Then moved backwards.

The Boy's Book of Railways shot from its shelf like a bullet, whizzing past her ear. She ducked. Other books followed, falling to the floor.

"Edward?" Ellie raised her voice. "That is you, isn't it? Edward Fitzberranger? Listen, Edward, I know who you are!"

There was silence.

Another book flew from the shelf. Ellie dodged as

Alice in Wonderland just missed her. She moved further into the room.

"Edward?"

On the far wall hung a large portrait – a golden-haired young woman in Victorian dress. Ellie jumped, as the boy suddenly stepped from behind the woman in the painting and floated down into the room.

"Edward, what is it? What's going on?"

Edward stared at her, blue eyes wide with fear.

"I think I'm being haunted."

Across the room, a vase suddenly shattered.

"Edward." Ellie spoke firmly. "Is this another one of your tricks?"

"No!" Edward insisted. "Someone's coming. Someone I can't hide from. And I mustn't be here when they arrive. Ellie, you must help me!"

Ellie hesitated. She fixed Edward with a stern look she'd borrowed from Mum.

"Why should I?"

"What?"

"Why should I help you?" Ellie said. "You haven't exactly made my life a bundle of fun since we got here –"

"Oh, don't be so *rotten*!" Edward looked quite spectacularly hurt. "What have *I* done?"

"What have –!" Ellie exploded. "Just – covering me with my own breakfast, so my family now thinks I'm loopy. Creeping out of everywhere and trying to scare me. Hurling me downstairs in the middle of the night –!"

Edward's mouth set into a sulky look.

"Well. I was only teasing."

Across the room, the piano lid suddenly rose, and fell with a crash.

Ellie stood with arms folded.

"All right, then. Apologise to me."

"What?"

"Apologise," Ellie said. "You Victorians were meant to be so polite. So let's have a proper Victorian apology."

She stared right into Edward's eyes.

"Now."

Edward stared back at her for a moment.

"Oh, crikey…"

Quickly, he gave Ellie something approaching a gentlemanly bow.

"I apologise, Miss Eleanor," he said stiffly. "What I did was unforgiveable. I do humbly and sincerely beg your pardon." He gave Ellie a sour look. "Will that do?"

"And what about my poetry?" Ellie asked.

Edward rolled his eyes.

"It's *wonderful*."

There was a pause.

Then Ellie smiled.

"OK. I'll help you. You can come down to our flat – if you don't think we're too common for you. Then you can tell me what's going on around here. Come on."

She made for the door.

She had left it open when she entered. But now it was shut. She tried to open it – and couldn't.

Something of the conceitedness returned to Edward's face.

"Not so clever after all, eh?"

Ellie gave him a narrow-eyed look.

"Well," Edward said. "At least *one* of us can get through."

"No!" Ellie yelled. "You can't leave me –"

Edward started to fade – and reappeared. He tried again to do his disappearing trick – and failed.

"You were saying?" Ellie asked.

"They're blocking me!" Edward reached for the door handle. His hand went straight through it. "We've got to get this door open!"

Ellie rattled the door.

"Someone's locked it!"

"It can't be locked!" Edward insisted. "I threw the key in the lake when I was seven…"

He stopped.

The tremors had ceased.

The toys fell to the floor. Everything was calm.

Upon the panelling of the door, a shadow was appearing.

It was the shadow of a woman.

A light, female voice came from beyond the door.

"Master Edward?"

"No…" Edward's voice sank into a whisper. "No, it can't be her! It can't!"

Very slowly, the door handle started to turn.

Chapter Seven

The door swung open.

"Ellie?" Mum stood in the doorway, frowning. "I thought I told you to get out of the house?"

Ellie blinked.

It wasn't Mum's voice she'd heard. But there was no one else in the corridor outside the nursery.

She turned to Edward.

He'd gone.

"Seems to have stopped, for the moment," Mum said. "It was really weird. Not like any earth tremor I've ever experienced."

She headed for the staircase.

"Come on. I need to go and rescue Marcus. He got trapped in the drawing room!"

Ellie remained. Everything was so still. But the scattered toys, the books were proof of what had happened.

She headed after Mum.

"So much for a quiet first day." Back in the flat, Mum moved to the table. The laptop had come back to life. "I see you've been researching, after all." She looked at the screen. "Who was Edward Fitzberranger?"

"Blind alley," Ellie said. She moved the mouse and closed the browser. "I thought it might lead me somewhere. It didn't." She paused. "Or at least, it hasn't yet."

"I'm pleased to see you behaving sensibly again." Mum turned away to the kitchen area. "I need a good strong coffee. Want some tea?"

"Thanks," Ellie said.

She sat down at the computer again. She'd have to go back to that website, as soon as Mum was out of the way.

What was the truth about Edward? From what she'd found, it looked as though he'd been right in saying this place was his.

But who was the woman they'd heard?

"Ellie!" a voice called.

Ellie jumped.

"What was that?" Mum asked, with her back turned.

"I didn't speak," Ellie said.

She looked at the computer. Her eyes bulged.

A new window had opened on the screen.

And standing in it, like a video clip, was Edward.

He gave her a little wave.

"Found something else?" Mum had seen the change in the screen display out of the corner of her eye. She turned back to the computer.

Ellie made a grab for the mouse and minimised the window.

"No," she said. "I mean – well – maybe. But I need

to check it out, first. I… think you might be surprised."

"Historical mystery, eh?" Mum passed a mug of tea to Ellie.

"Something like that." Ellie cringed, as a strange noise came from deep within the computer.

It sounded like someone saying: *Oi!*

"That's strange." Mum reached over, tapping a couple of keys experimentally. "Don't recognise that sound. Maybe the quake's affected it."

The computer shook slightly.

"Perhaps I'd better call Technical Support," Mum said.

"I think it's OK." Ellie directed her voice to the computer. "I think maybe something just needs *booting up*."

"Well, let me know if there are any more problems." Mum gulped her coffee. "I'd better get back to the office. If you find out any more historical stuff you can start writing some text for the guidebook, if you like."

"Thanks," Ellie said.

She waited until the green baize door had closed after Mum.

Then she maximised the window again.

"That's a nice thing to do." Edward reappeared on the screen, looking indignant. "Squashing a fellow. What is this thing I'm in, anyway?"

"It's a computer," Ellie said. "We use them for all kinds of things. Writing letters. Doing sums. Looking things up…"

"Father had one of those," Edward said. "He was

called a secretary." He sniffed. "You think you're so clever, you people. In my time, we ruled the world. And we didn't need computators, or moving telephones, or those great noisy flying machines that keep coming overhead…"

"Planes," Ellie said. "And I think you mean mobiles." She grinned. "Are you coming out of there, then, or do I have to download you?"

Edward grimaced. He disappeared from the screen.

The next moment, he was standing by Ellie's side.

"Hmm." He gave the computer a dirty look. "You know your trouble? Your generation? You're spoiled."

He adjusted his collar.

"You can't know anything about it!" Ellie said. "I mean, you can't have *seen* any of the things that have happened since your time, not properly. You were just a –"

She stared at Edward.

"You were just a boy."

She stopped.

She remembered the words she'd seen on the Internet.

No surviving male heir…

And for the first time, she realised properly what a child's ghost must mean.

There was a very long silence.

Finally, Ellie said, quietly:

"How?"

Edward avoided her gaze.

"Scarlet fever."

Ellie hesitated.

"How old were you?"

Edward looked down at the table.

"Ten."

Ellie blinked.

"I'm sorry."

There was another silence.

"I didn't know it had happened at first," Edward said eventually. "That's the odd thing. I'd been lying in bed for days. Doctor said I was starting to get better.

'Morning came… I remember the clock along the passage striking seven. It was spring. The trees were in leaf, I could see them through the window. I thought: as soon as I'm well again, I'm going out there. I'll climb that tallest tree, right to the very top. I'd always been meaning to. I lay there for a while, then… without knowing it, I was out of bed, standing in the room. I thought Mother would be so pleased, to see me up and about. Then she came in. I was smiling.

'"Mother!" I said."

He paused.

"And then I realised she couldn't hear me."

He turned to Ellie. Their eyes met.

"The next thing, she had Father in there, and my sister, and a couple of the servants. And then I looked back at the bed.

'And I saw myself, still lying there.

'And then Father said:

'"He's gone.""

He stopped.

"I tried to tell them I hadn't. But no one was listening."

Ellie caught her breath.

Instinctively, she went over and put her arm around Edward's shoulders. It went straight through him.

"Edward. I'm so sorry."

"Oh…" Edward tried to push her away, with no more success. "It all happened years and years ago. It happened a lot, in those days. And of course, my darling sister and her foul husband got the estate, with me gone."

"And you've been here ever since?" Ellie asked.

"All through the years," Edward answered. "All through the wars, the first one, and the second when more of those beastly noisy things started appearing in the sky. I've seen decades of rotten Harveys here, while our name died with Father. Though there *were* some other children here, in the second war especially." He brightened, momentarily. "Horrid young things from London. I had a jolly good time scaring them. They were even more fun than you."

His face darkened again.

"But I always knew I shouldn't really still be here. And that's where *she* –"

He stopped.

"Edward?" Ellie asked. "Who is she?"

"Hello, Shakespeare. Not finished work yet?"

Ellie jumped.

Charlie was standing beside her.

On her other side, there was no one to be seen.

"Not found anything?" Charlie looked at the empty computer screen. "You should stick to painting. Leave running a business to the people in the know. You'd better clear this away. Mum wants to start lunch."

Ellie could have kicked him.

Ellie saw no more of Edward that afternoon, or evening. She was starting to feel oddly bored, when he wasn't there.

She sent another text to Dad, and had a reply. It just said: *Still* ♥ *u*.

She wrote some paragraphs for the children's guidebook and showed them to Mum.

When bedtime came, Ellie found herself lying awake again.

It must have been awful, for Edward. Being in this house for years and years, seeing other people living in the home that should have been yours.

She still didn't know who that voice had belonged to.

Eventually, the exhaustion of the day overtook her, and she fell into a deep sleep.

"Miss Eleanor?"

Ellie sat up in bed.

But it wasn't her bed.

She found herself in one of the upper rooms of the house, a bedroom, comfortably surrounded by soft sheets, bolsters and pillows.

She stared around her. The room was beautifully

furnished, and much grander than the faded rooms were today. She could make out a dressing-table, and a vase of red tulips on the mantelpiece.

She looked out of the window. It was daylight outside. She could see the tops of the chestnut trees, just as Edward had described them. Yet inside the room, it was still dark.

She looked down. She was wearing a Victorian nightgown, in embroidered silk.

The door of the room was opening.

And she recognised the voice outside.

"Miss Eleanor?" the voice repeated. "It's time for you to wake up."

"Who are you?" Ellie demanded. "And why do you want Edward?"

There was a light, female laugh.

"Master Edward's playtime is over," the voice said. "It's time he was resting. While you… still have a great deal to learn."

The door swung open in a blaze of light.

And for the first time, Ellie saw the owner of the voice.

The woman who appeared was young. She might once have been pretty, but her face was now hard and severe, with her fair hair tied back tightly. She wore a white blouse, and a black skirt that was so long it hid her feet and made her appear to float.

Under her arm, she carried a large book.

"This is wrong." Ellie's mind worked fast. "I'm not Victorian, I'm from now. There's nothing you can teach me –"

She stopped, and stared at the young woman. The clothes… the book… she had seen very old photos of women dressed like that.

"Teach me…" Ellie repeated. "Of course. You're a governess!"

Her eyes widened.

"Edward's teacher… That's why he was so scared of you!"

"What a clever young lady you are," the woman remarked. "If only I had taught someone like you. I might have been happy. None of this might ever have occurred."

"What do you mean?"

The woman made no reply to this, but took up the book she carried.

She opened it, and started to read.

"Edward James John Fitzberranger. Passed over, Eighteen Hundred and Ninety-Seven. Record of Conduct. Eighteen Hundred and Ninety-Eight – Misuse of Spiritual Powers to scare two children visiting the house, both much younger than himself. Later that year, using powers to unfix the stair carpet, causing three people to fall."

She turned the page.

"Eighteen Hundred and Ninety-Nine, overturning a pudding basin onto a kitchen-maid."

She turned further pages.

"Buckets of water… motor cars interfered with… right up to yourself, yesterday. Master Edward really has been very wicked."

She smiled.

"You should be careful with whom you associate. One day, one of these will be written about you."

"He's never done anything evil!" Ellie said. She didn't know that at all, but felt oddly bound to protect her friend. "He just likes having fun."

Quickly, she scrambled out of bed and stepped right up to the governess.

"What do you want with him? And why now?"

She forced herself to meet the governess's eyes. They were a steely grey.

"I'm not going to let you harm him."

"You still don't understand, do you?" the governess said. "No matter. So be it. I had hoped to persuade you to be good. But if you persist –"

Another object appeared in her hand. Ellie paled.

It was a cane.

"Remember," the governess continued. "This is the Victorian age. If you spare the rod, you spoil the child. We know, in these days, how to make children behave."

Ellie squared her shoulders.

"I'm not afraid of you."

"Very well," the governess finished. "But I shall be there. Watching you. When you least expect it. And very soon – you and Master Edward will do exactly as you're told."

With that, she began to fade, drifting back towards the door.

And Ellie found herself drifting too, back into the bed, before seeing the mantelpiece, and the tulips, and the richly-papered bedroom walls moving further and further away from her…

Ellie blinked.

"Ellie?" Mum shouted. "Aren't you up yet? I've got a crisis on, out here!"

A shaft of sunlight shone through the scullery door. Ellie grabbed her watch. It was eight a.m.

There was something else by the bed, as well… something red. Ellie grasped it and lifted it into view.

It was a tulip.

Chapter Eight

Ellie dressed hastily and made her way out into the kitchen area. Mum and Charlie were there, already finishing breakfast. Charlie was wearing his best purple shirt and patterned tie, and his hair was looking particularly gelled and shaped.

"Got a date, Charlie?" Ellie sniggered. "What's going on?"

"Spot check," Mum answered. "Head Office is doing a swoop on us."

She was looking smart too, in a navy blue suit. She rose from the table and bustled around the flat, grabbing her badge and a clipboard from nearby chairs.

"Typical Journeyback. We're nowhere near ready for this, yet."

Ellie yawned. After a night arguing with a ghost, she wasn't ready for the world of Journeyback either.

"What do you mean, spot check?"

Charlie straightened his tie.

"At eleven o'clock, they're sending a sample coach party to see over the place. Not a real one, of course. They use members of staff, a few volunteers – and a few members of the public to make it seem real. They get a free day out."

"And that means," Mum said. "That everything has to be absolutely perfect. This despite the fact we've no staff here yet. Marcus and I have got to do everything ourselves. They want to see what sort of a welcome we'll give to visitors. Then we'll give them coffee and biscuits in the library." She turned to Charlie. "You're making the coffee. There won't be many people. Only a dozen or so."

The look of superiority vanished from Charlie's face.

"A shame we didn't have your guidebook done, Ellie," Mum went on. "At least we'd have had one bit of quality to show them."

Ellie directed a virtuous smile in Charlie's direction. He scowled.

Mum stopped in the act of scooping up paperwork. She looked at Ellie.

"You've not even had any breakfast, yet."

"Don't worry, Mum." Ellie moved to the table. "I can get my own. I'll clear, too."

She took a careful look at the ketchup bottle and milk carton.

"I'll make sure everything's clean and tidy."

Mum paused.

"OK." She headed for the door. "Come on, Charlie. Start practising your best professional smile."

Charlie drew his face into a ferocious grin.

As soon as they'd gone, Ellie looked cautiously around the flat.

"Edward?"

There was silence.

"Edward, I've seen her! I know who she is!"

There was no response.

Frowning, Ellie started to clear Mum and Charlie's breakfast things.

A governess... so Edward had been educated at home. She knew lots of rich kids were, in those days. Then they'd go away to boarding school. The boys, at least.

The governess had been young. Did that mean she was still young when she died?

What about the book? It contained a record. Of all the people Edward had frightened. All the bad things he'd done.

The governess had certainly been scary. But why was Edward so afraid of her?

And why had she only just appeared to him, after such a long time?

Ellie stationed herself inside the entrance to the Manor when eleven o'clock arrived.

A coach made its way up the drive, and a group of people emerged onto the gravel.

Ellie smiled to herself. Mum was out there, professional smile in place. Marcus was all hearty greeting and was trying to shake hands with twelve people at once. Charlie was attempting to do the same, and was being ignored.

The visitors were an interesting mix of people. There was a silver-haired man in a suit who was receiving a lot of Marcus's attention and looked like he might be the boss… a couple of old ladies wearing Journeyback Volunteer badges… and a dark-haired young woman, appearing from behind the coach, who was looking up at the Manor with fascination.

Ellie dodged back towards their flat, out of sight, as the visitors made their way into the house.

She smiled to herself. She was becoming very good at hiding.

It must be all the time she was spending with Edward.

"What do you mean, they've gone?"

Ellie tapped on the door of the Site Office and entered. It was a bright and cheerful room, with a cast-iron fireplace, a patterned carpet and very high windows. The housekeepers of Inchwood had enjoyed an excellent view of the courtyard below. Marcus's changes to the room consisted of one desk, one computer and one phone.

Charlie was sitting at the desk, looking sulky. Marcus had gone the colour of pickled cabbage. He gestured towards some empty chairs.

"Three coats, two bags, an umbrella, a fur hat and a copy of *Historic Houses Weekly* can't just disappear!" He glared at Charlie. "You were meant to stay and keep an eye on things here, while your mother and I took everyone round the house!"

"If any of the loos worked up here…" Charlie cut in.

"Now, you listen to me, mister –" Marcus started. He spun round to see Ellie there. "Yes?"

Ellie smiled charmingly.

"Where's Mum?"

"Downstairs," Marcus said. "Holding the fort, while I try to locate most of our visitors' personal belongings, which your clever brother has somehow lost from right under his nose!"

Ellie paused.

"I'll have a look for them," she said.

She didn't have to look far. Sure enough, when she entered the nursery, there they were, scattered about all over the place. Edward's rocking horse was wearing the hat, while she could see small, torn pictures from *Historic Houses Weekly* as posters on the railway station of Edward's train set.

"Edward?" Ellie grabbed items as best she could. "You're not funny, you know. Hey, you want to be careful. *She*'s still out there. She's taking notes. And…" She paused. "I've seen her. Last night. I know who she is, now."

There was no answer.

"Edward!" Ellie moved across the nursery. She looked at all the places Edward might be hiding… the paintings… a half-open cupboard… behind the curtains. "Look, she's got it all written down! Everything you've done. She's looking for you. But I still don't know why. Edward, if you tell me what's going on, maybe I can help!"

Silence.

Ellie waited a moment. Then she gave up.

She emerged from the room, her arms full, to meet Mum coming upstairs.

"Ah!" Mum smiled. "You've found them. Good. I knew they couldn't have gone far."

She leaned closer to Ellie.

"I suppose it's no good asking how they got in there? Get all that stuff downstairs, now. And whatever you do, just keep smiling."

Someone was coming upstairs behind Mum... the dark-haired young woman Ellie had seen earlier.

"This is Moira," Mum said. She gestured downward. "Go *on*, Ellie!"

Ellie moved to the stairs. She heard snatches of conversation floating after her.

"Moira's interested in volunteering with us... admin..."

"I've just graduated." The young woman had a gentle, pleasant voice. "History. I've been looking for some voluntary work..."

Keen to meet the new arrival, Ellie went back to the Site Office after returning the stolen property. The visitors were now in the library, doing their best to enjoy Charlie's coffee.

Marcus obviously wasn't wasting any time. Moira was already wearing a Volunteer badge. She was seated at the desk.

"Well, I've worked in University offices," she was saying. "During the holidays. And I promise you, you won't find a better letter-writer anywhere." She caught sight of Ellie. "Hello."

"I'm Ellie," Ellie said, since no one had introduced her. "That was my Mum you met before."

"You can use a computer, I suppose, Moira?" Marcus banged the monitor with his hand.

"Yes." Moira glanced at the machine. "Of course."

"Perhaps you wouldn't mind starting with a letter to catering, then," Marcus said. "Details on the desk. I've got to get downstairs. Try and repair the damage the *rest* of my workforce have done this morning." He headed for the door. "Do it yourself, Marcus…"

For the first time, Ellie met Moira's gaze.

Both of them stifled a smile.

As soon as Marcus had gone, Ellie took a chair beside the desk. She needed a friend, around here. Someone who couldn't walk through walls.

"So," Moira said. "What's it like, living in a place this size?"

"It's cool," Ellie said. "We only moved in two days ago."

She paused. Making new friends always made her strangely nervous. She was never sure what to say. She cleared her throat.

"Did you say you've just come back from uni?"

"Yes," Moira said. "Cambridge."

"Wow," Ellie said. "And you end up working for Marcus."

Moira laughed. She brushed her hair back from her soft, grey eyes.

"I wasn't expecting to start work so quickly. My mother thinks I'm only out for the morning. She's expecting me back for lunch. You know mothers."

"Oh!" Ellie laughed. It was the first time she remembered laughing since coming to Inchwood. "Tell me about it!"

She stopped as she heard floorboards creak in the corridor outside – then, footsteps heading downstairs.

She moved quickly to the door and opened it. As expected, there was no one in sight.

She turned back to Moira.

"Just got to pop down, sorry. I'll see you later. I've got to… go and find someone…"

"Oh?" Moira asked. "Who's that?"

Ellie was already heading for the ground floor.

"I reckon Moira's just what we're looking for," Marcus was saying to Mum, at the main entrance. "And she's local. She can bus it over here – any day, she said."

He noted Ellie's arrival. Charlie had also appeared, and was carefully standing a short distance from Marcus, doing his best to look dignified.

"Anyway. Spot check successful. We can go and see 'em off, now."

Ellie followed Mum and Marcus as they stepped out into the courtyard and approached the group of visitors. Nearby, a young man was watering some hydrangeas with a hose. He looked bored and sheepish and his badge showed he was another volunteer.

Marcus looked at him proudly.

"That's the stuff, Clay," he said, loudly enough for the visitors to hear. "Now, ladies and gentlemen, on behalf of the Journeyback team here at Inchwood, can I just say how much we've valued your creative input today. And when we open, later this summer, I can promise you that this is how we will welcome visitors to this great house."

Ellie stared.

The young man seemed to be fighting with the hose. It was twitching… shifting…

She watched as it flew out of his hand and snaked its way across the gravel.

Marcus turned and saw it coming just too late.

There were shrieks, and yells, and running, as everyone tried to get out of the way. The boss's expensive suit was saturated. Charlie's shirt and tie were soaked and his carefully-gelled hair was plastered to his forehead. The old ladies were grimly hanging onto their hats.

"Clay!" Marcus bellowed. He was whirling about, in the centre of the storm, trying to work out what was going on. "Turn it off!"

"I can't!" the volunteer shouted back. "It's stuck!"

Ellie decided to leave the adults alone with this one.

As she went back into the house, she noted with pleasure that she was completely dry.

Edward must be starting to like her.

Chapter Nine

Mum and Charlie got themselves dry. Marcus changed his suit. He then made a very awkward phone call to Head Office.

After lunch, more volunteers started to arrive – mostly locals that Marcus had managed to recruit in the village along with Clay.

"You'd be surprised what buying a few pints at the local pub can do," he said to Mum.

The villagers lost some of their enthusiasm when they discovered exactly what Marcus wanted.

"All the rubbish to be cleared out," he told them, as he took them through the upper rooms of the Manor. "This place has got to look spic and span. But watch out. Some of this stuff could be valuable. Come to me if there's any doubts."

Later in the afternoon, Ellie stole upstairs for another chat with Moira.

The Site Office was stacked with objects. The villagers had evidently had several doubts. A hideous brass table-lamp stood on top of a woodworm-ridden chest of drawers, with an old and rusty bicycle parked alongside. There were several mouldering old books, and dozens of cardboard boxes of junk.

Ellie thought that Miss Harvey couldn't have had a clear-out in quite a while.

"Strange, isn't it?" Moira broke into Ellie's thoughts. "These old houses. The things that get cast aside."

"I could do some good abstracts of this stuff." Ellie studied the pile of rubbish. "Or even enter it for something as it is. As a piece of contemporary art."

"You paint, do you?" Moira asked.

"Yeah," Ellie said. "And I write poetry, sometimes."

"I used to paint," Moira said. "A little. I'd be interested to see some of your paintings. You could work up here. Keep me company."

"Sure," Ellie agreed. "I'd like to do the view from this window."

She was interrupted as the office door opened.

Marcus entered. He was dishing out orders to people in the corridor behind him.

"Just pile it all up, we'll sort the good stuff out…"

"Do you think this could be antique?" a ginger-bearded young man asked.

Ellie stifled a snigger. It was the same kind of standard lamp she remembered Mum and Dad having when she was little.

"I don't think so, somehow." Even Marcus looked amused. "No good to us. Unless we're going to have an Eighties night."

"And what about this?" another villager asked.

Ellie looked at the next object – and froze.

It was a small, framed portrait of Edward.

"Dunno," Marcus admitted. "Let's ask our

historian." He turned to the desk. "What d'you make of this, Moira?"

"I'm no expert." Moira got up and looked at the painting nonetheless. Ellie followed.

It was a good likeness. Edward was about the same age in the picture as he appeared now. It must have been painted not long before he became ill. He was wearing what might have been his best suit, with a high, gleaming white collar, and even in the picture he looked as if he were already planning some mischief.

"Victorian, I'd say," Moira said. "Judging by the clothes." She looked at the base of the frame. "No inscription."

"Not exactly Rembrandt, is it?" Marcus took a closer look. "Biscuit-box stuff." He flicked at the picture lightly with his fingers.

Ellie blinked, as she heard a faint sound.

It sounded like: *Ow!*

Quickly, she stepped forward.

"The paintings in the nursery look a bit like that," she said. "Maybe they're the work of the same artist."

Marcus looked doubtful.

"If you say so."

"Maybe we could put it on display in there?" Ellie went on. "You know… a child… in a nursery… This boy might even have played there."

Marcus shrugged.

"Fine. Stick it in there, for now. There's loads of stuff we need to get valued, anyway."

Ellie took a firm hold of the portrait.

As soon as she was inside the nursery, she placed the portrait carefully on a chair.

"OK. I know you're in there. Come out."

"You're no fun any more," Edward said. "You keep finding me. I bet you're *rotten* to play Hide and Seek with."

He stepped into view from behind his image in the painting. For a moment, there were two Edwards within the frame. Then, the talking one stepped out into the room.

"And what does "OK" mean?"

"We've got to talk," Ellie said. "I saw that woman. Last night. In a dream… I think."

Edward frowned.

"Good job I found this thing." He indicated the portrait. "Father had this done for Mother's birthday. I had to stand still for *hours*. Ghastly, isn't it?"

"It's very like you, though," Ellie said.

Edward ignored this.

"I'm glad you got hold of it," he said. "Because it's your help I need, to escape from *her*."

"What do you mean?" Ellie asked.

"Simple," Edward said. "The house isn't safe for me, any more. I can't just vanish, if I use my powers to escape *she'll* know. That's why *you're* going to get me out of here."

He went to the window and pointed downward.

"I heard your mother. She's going down to the

village. All I have to do is hide inside the portrait. And you can smuggle me out in your motor car."

"Hang on!" Ellie did her best to keep up. "How am I meant to carry that thing out of here, without being spotted? And into our car? The painting's probably worth something. They'll think I'm nicking it!"

"*Nicking…?*" Edward pondered.

"Stealing it," Ellie translated. "No, I'm sorry, Edward. No way am I doing something like that."

Just before Mum was due to leave for the village, Ellie exited the house as quietly as she could. There was no one around.

She was holding her portfolio, which contained some of her own paintings.

She opened the folder slightly.

"Are you all right in there?" she whispered.

"No," whinged a familiar voice from within. "It's dark in here! And it smells! Why do you use oils? What was wrong with watercolours?"

"You know," Ellie told him. "Even for a ghost, you do a lot of moaning."

She looked around. The portrait wasn't large, but it was really too big to be held by the portfolio, frame and all. She only hoped Mum wouldn't look at it too closely.

And what was she going to do with Edward, once they got to the village?

"We're lucky they haven't got the security system in yet," she muttered into the folder.

"Talking to yourself?" Charlie's voice said. Ellie

whirled round. "Knew you were going round the twist. Soon as I saw you covered in ketchup yesterday."

Ellie groaned inwardly. This was all she needed.

"What are you doing here?"

"Coming down the village with Mum." Charlie took his phone from his belt. "There's got to be somewhere to top this up. Gonna try the village store."

He examined the portfolio.

"What you brought this for?"

"Get off!" Ellie pulled it away. "If you must know. I thought there might be some interesting subjects down there."

Charlie sniggered.

"You do remember the village?" He made for the front passenger seat of the car. "Come on then, small person. Get in."

Ellie clambered into the back seat, holding the portfolio carefully.

Mum emerged from the house, shopping bags at the ready. She was looking at a list.

"Need more milk, butter, cheese, bananas, something for supper, courgettes to make ratatouille on Saturday…"

She settled herself in the driving seat.

"This is jolly!" whispered Edward. "There used to be some splendid parties here, just after my time. People came in motor cars… lovely picnic baskets…"

"Ssh!" Ellie told him.

"Did you say something?" Mum asked.

Ellie made a hasty show of coughing.

"No. Something caught my throat."

"What kind of motor is this?" the voice went on. "And who's got the starting-handle?"

"If you don't shut up…." Ellie hissed.

"I didn't *speak*!" Charlie yelled. "Mum… she's being weird again!"

"If you don't *both* stop it – now – I'll leave you here," Mum said.

She turned the ignition key. Nothing happened.

"That's weird." Mum tried again, and again. The engine wasn't turning over at all.

"Told you!" chirped a voice from inside the portfolio. "You need the handle!"

Ellie thumped it.

"Ow!"

"Did you hear a kind of weird noise, just then?" Charlie asked. "I reckon it's an electrical fault."

"This car's not going anywhere," Mum said. "Sorry, kids. You'd better get out."

With looks of annoyance, Ellie and Charlie emerged from the car.

As an afterthought, Mum tried the key once more.

The engine started.

"Oh." Mum sounded surprised. "Right. Back on board."

Charlie got back into the car. So did Ellie.

And a moment later, the engine cut out again.

"That's so strange." Mum turned the key. "It was all right until you two got in."

"Weightload." Charlie switched to another scientific

theory. "Something to do with the suspension."

Ellie frowned.

Then she realised.

"Hang on, Mum." She stepped out of the car, with the portfolio. "Now try."

Mum tried again. And the engine burst into life.

Charlie laughed.

"I knew it! Ellie's cursed! Or her paintings are."

"I think you'd both better stay here," Mum said. "Until I get this car looked at. There's a garage, just the other side of the village."

Charlie's face fell. He took a last, agonised look at his phone.

Ellie smiled.

"I should have known!" Edward's voice whined, as soon as Ellie re-entered the hall.

Ellie took the painting from the portfolio. Edward stepped into view within the frame, beside himself in every sense.

Ellie had worked out the answer too.

"You can't leave?"

"There's a barrier on me!" Edward groaned. "I should have realised. It's how they keep me where I'm meant to be. Until…"

He fell silent.

"Until what?" Ellie asked. "Look, Edward. I really think it's time you told me what's going on."

"Oh, so that's where it got to." Marcus appeared from the drawing room.

Ellie's heart leapt.

In another second, Edward had jumped back into the picture.

"I thought you were going out?" Marcus went on. "No worries. I'll take it back upstairs."

He made a grab for the painting.

"No…" Ellie protested.

Marcus looked at the portrait he was holding. "Ugly little brat, isn't he?"

He winced.

"You all right?" Ellie asked.

"Cramp." Marcus rubbed his hand. "Weird. Felt like someone pinching me…"

He headed for the stairs.

Ellie went back to the flat, to think.

It was OK. Marcus would put the portrait back in the nursery. But there were still masses of volunteers upstairs. Edward would just have to hide out a bit longer.

She'd been so close to learning the truth. So Edward was trapped – in the house – or at least on the estate. But what did his governess want with him?

And why now?

"Where's the portrait?" Ellie came out of the nursery in a hurry. "Where's Marcus?"

She nearly ran straight into Moira.

"Moira! That portrait – the one the boy was in. I mean, the one of the boy. It's not in the nursery – where is it?"

"I haven't –" Moira started.

Ellie entered the Site Office. Volunteers were there, starting to remove the junk. But there was no sign of Edward's picture.

She had to find Marcus!

Ellie emerged from the house.

She stopped. She could smell something.

Smoke…

She moved rapidly onward. She recognised that smell, from the allotments near their old home.

She rounded a corner of the house.

Two of the men from the village had built a bonfire. They were throwing on all sorts of things… bits of garden waste… wood… newspaper…

And in the centre of the fire, Edward was burning inside his frame.

The oil paint was an easy target for the flames, and the canvas was already disintegrating. Edward's suit blackened and smouldered. His face was charring… disappearing…

Ellie buried her face in her hands.

Chapter Ten

"Two mess-ups in one day!" Mum was laughing on her return from the village. "That's a record, even for Marcus."

She addressed Charlie, who was at the computer.

"You know that painting he was going on about? The Victorian boy? Two of those local volunteers only went and chucked him on a bonfire!"

She hung up her coat and bag.

"The thing is, these volunteers claim they were following Marcus's instructions. But we couldn't even discipline them, find out what really happened, because dear old Marcus...didn't do the paperwork! He hadn't actually signed them up yet! So these two just stormed off, taking most of the other volunteers with them. He won't be able to set foot in that pub again!"

She looked at Ellie, who was sitting near Charlie at the table, slowly leafing through her crumpled poems.

"Well, I thought it was funny." She opened her shopping bags. "What do you want for tea, then?"

"Not bothered, thanks," Ellie answered.

She dropped the poems lightly onto the tabletop.

"I'm not really hungry."

After a mostly silent meal, Ellie disappeared.

Mum found her upstairs, alone in the nursery. She was looking at the train set, which still had the torn magazine pictures on the station... giving the horse a gentle rock... flicking through *The Boy's Book of Railways*...

"All right," Mum said. Ellie jumped. "What's wrong?"

There was silence.

"I'm not still cross with you, you know," Mum said. "About yesterday. I was only surprised because it was so unlike you."

A pause.

"Do you really hate it here?" Mum asked.

Ellie shook her head. She looked out of the window, at the tallest tree Edward had been planning to climb.

"You'll be starting your new school next week," Mum went on. "You're bound to make some new friends."

She hesitated.

"And I've got a surprise for you. Saturday, your Dad's coming, for lunch."

Ellie brightened a little.

"Meanwhile," Mum said. "It's my day off tomorrow. Marcus is off to Head Office. Why don't we do something, as a family? You and Charlie have been cooped up in the house for two days now. We could go to the lake. Explore a bit. Did I hear you talking about having a picnic there?"

"Yes." Ellie managed to force a smile for her Mum. "OK... cool."

"Coming back downstairs, then?"

Ellie followed slowly.

She took a last, long look around the nursery. This room had scared her, that first night. So had Edward. But now, she was longing to hear the piano playing itself, or see the train moving off on a new journey.

The whole place was like a tomb.

At noon the following day, Ellie set off from the house with Mum and Charlie. Mum was carrying the cool-box containing their provisions. Charlie had been loaded up with rugs and a folding picnic table and was doing his long-suffering act.

Ellie had her sketchbook and camera. There might be some interesting subjects. Though she wasn't really in the mood to think about sketches or paintings.

They arrived at the main entrance to see Moira approaching across the gravel.

"Hello, everyone!" She noted Charlie's huge stack of luggage. "Going out?"

"We thought we'd go for a picnic down by the lake." Mum paused. "Join us, if you like. Marcus is away 'til tonight. If he asks, I'll tell him it was work experience for you. Outdoor Education."

Moira laughed.

"Thanks."

"I could show you some of my work, too," Ellie said.

"Come on, then," Mum said. "There's plenty of food for four. I just hope you like tinned salmon."

She led the way.

A few minutes' walk took them through the rose garden, across the lawns and beyond the trees.

Ellie stared. The lake was vast, surrounded by weeping willows and thick clumps of reeds.

The spot they chose for their picnic gave them a view of the island. Ellie gazed at it across the gently rippling water. In contrast to the lake, the island was small. But the folly was impressive – a sort of temple, with pillars and a domed roof…

"Hey." Mum's voice entered Ellie's thoughts. "Come on, daydreamer. Never mind the poetic muse – I've got a picnic to set up, here!"

Ellie pulled her thoughts back. The rugs and table were already in place and she helped Mum and Moira to set out the sandwiches.

Ellie ate little. Everywhere she looked, it was as though she could see Edward… playing by the water's edge… maybe enjoying a picnic here with his family, in those far-off days.

Now, all the family was gone.

"Anyway," Moira said. "When I got back to the college, two of the other students, Brandon and George…"

"Brandon?" Ellie was smiling.

"They'd unscrewed the hinges of all the doors," Moira went on. "Including the bathroom. I came back, and there was a bathroom door right across the passageway. With my rooms on the other side. I thought I'd have to camp out in the lobby."

Ellie met Moira's eye. Then both of them burst out laughing.

Ellie wiped the tears away. "You're mad!"

They were sitting in the mid-afternoon sun, enjoying the view and the dappled shade of the trees.

Charlie was fast asleep on a rug. Mum was busy packing away the last of the picnic things. She cast a glance in the girls' direction.

"Perhaps we should be getting back."

"There's no hurry, is there?" Ellie asked. She turned back to Moira. "Tell me some more."

"You said Marcus would be away all day, Judith," Moira said. She glanced at Charlie. "Perhaps *he's* got the right idea. Why don't *you* have a little rest, as well?"

Mum paused. Then she leaned back against a tree.

"Suppose you're right. It is my day off, after all."

Moira picked up Ellie's sketchbook.

"You know, these are good. You have talent."

She stood up and headed for the water's edge.

"Coming for a walk?"

Ellie rose and followed Moira. They took another look across to the island. The folly seemed so near.

"Hey," Moira said. "Look."

She pointed to something that was half-hidden by weeds at the edge of the lake. A dirty white-painted hull and part of an oar were just visible.

"It's a boat!"

A minute or so later, Ellie and Moira had managed to part the weeds so that the entire boat came into view. It looked old, and much-used, but sturdy.

"I can row," Moira said.

"I bet we could row across to the island." Ellie looked round. "We could, couldn't we, Mum… Mum?"

A tiny snore answered her question from beneath the tree.

Ellie turned back to Moira. They exchanged glances.

Moira made a careful examination of the hull of the boat and the oars.

Then she gave a nod to Ellie.

Moira proved a good oarswoman as well as a careful one. Soon, they were skimming across the water, with a cool breeze blowing in their faces.

Ellie gave Moira an admiring glance.

She felt excited, though nervous too. She knew, deep down, that Mum would never have agreed to this.

"Charlie said your father's coming tomorrow," Moira said. "That'll be nice for you."

Ellie turned her face further into the breeze.

"You seemed unhappy earlier," Moira went on. "It isn't easy, is it? When families break up, go their different ways?"

"No," Ellie said. She looked back at Moira. "Have you been through that, as well?"

There was a pause. Then Moira nodded.

"My father left my mother when I was very small. Then, later, my mother became ill. And I was forced to go out to work."

She stopped rowing for a moment.

"I'd done well, at school. I was expected to go on to great things."

"You made it to Cambridge –" Ellie started.

Her voice trailed off as she stared across the lake.

Something was covering the waters on the far side – a kind of haze. You didn't get mist on lakes in the middle of a bright sunny day.

Through the haze, she could just make out an object – white-painted.

It was a boat, just like their own.

Two figures were in the boat. A white-suited young man with long, dark hair and a beard, and a young woman with tied-back hair, a white blouse and a long skirt.

The man was fooling about, pretending he couldn't row. The woman was laughing.

As quickly as it had come, the vision disappeared, leaving a clear day and a cool expanse of lake, with no other boat to be seen.

"Are you all right, Ellie?" Moira asked.

Ellie blinked.

"Yeah… yeah. I'm fine."

She gazed across the water.

They reached their destination shortly afterwards. Moira found a stout wooden post at the edge of the island, where they tied up the boat. People living at the Manor had obviously made this journey in the past.

"Let's explore," said Ellie. "Get some photos. 'Long

as I don't let Mum see them." She paused. "We'd better get back soon."

She took the digital camera from her pocket and switched it on. If only she'd had it at the ready a few minutes ago!

"Come on then." She dodged among the pillars of the folly. She headed for a wide slab, mounted on a stone block, which formed the centrepiece. It looked like a kind of table. She hoisted herself up onto it.

She held the camera out to Moira.

"Will you take one of me? It's all set up."

Moira took the camera and slowly examined its controls.

"I knew it!" Ellie grinned. "I've come out here with a technophobe." She lowered herself down from the slab. "Tell you what, we'll use the timer."

She took the camera back and made a few adjustments. She placed the camera on top of the slab, and went to stand next to Moira.

"Now we can both be in it." Ellie beamed. Then she glanced sideways. Moira was looking rather solemn. "Come on, smile!"

Moira smiled awkwardly.

There was a click from the camera.

"Let's get some on the mobile." Ellie switched her phone on. "I can text them to Dad." She held the phone high and took a picture of them both, then another.

Abruptly, Moira moved away.

"Let's go and see the other side of the island," she suggested. She went to the slab and picked up the camera. "I'll take this. There are some fine views from there."

She disappeared around the perimeter of the folly.

Ellie frowned. She stood for a moment, staring back across the water.

She shivered. It was surprisingly cold, around this old, stone building. She had the feeling that she was trespassing. It felt like no one had been on this island for years.

"Did you find anything?" she called.

There was silence.

"Moira?"

Ellie stepped out of the folly. She walked around to the rear.

"Moira? Moira!"

In less than thirty seconds, she had covered the whole island, in and around the folly.

There was no sign of her friend.

Chapter Eleven

Ellie ran back to where they'd tied up the boat.

It was still there. Moira couldn't have left that way.

She ran around the island again. This was insane.

She skidded to a halt.

"Oh, Edward," she muttered. "Why didn't you tell me? What's going on?"

All at once, she felt exhausted. She went and sat on the cold, stone slab.

She didn't know how long she remained like that, utterly miserable. The sun had disappeared behind a big, black cloud, and the wind was growing colder. It would be raining soon.

She couldn't even see Mum, or Charlie. The mist seemed to have closed in again, and was shrouding the other side of the lake from view. She tried shouting. But there was no reply.

She took her phone from her pocket. There was no signal.

She wondered what they'd do, when they found her gone.

Ellie hadn't got beyond the ten metres badge for swimming. And she'd seen that the oars of the boat would be way too heavy for her.

What had happened to Moira? She surely wouldn't just abandon her. But how could Moira have got off the island at all?

Ellie frowned, as she remembered her vision… the other boat…. the woman.

She was sure the woman had been the governess.

Why had Edward been so afraid of her? Could she be responsible for Moira's disappearance?

She remembered the dream – and the governess's words.

"*You and Master Edward will do exactly as you're told.*"

"You're on your own now, Ellie," she told herself. "On your own. Against *her*."

She shifted uncomfortably on the slab. She wobbled suddenly, almost losing her balance.

The slab was loose!

She scrambled down to ground level, placed her hands on the slab and pushed.

It was heavy. But slowly, steadily, it moved, revealing a black, empty space below.

Ellie retched. The air beneath was stale and dank. No one could have moved this slab for decades.

She pushed further, until a deep pit was revealed.

"Boo!"

A small, blond head popped out, jack-in-the-box style, from the black space and a familiar impudent grin appeared.

"About time, too," said a cheerful, smug voice. "What kept you?"

Ellie gawped.

"Edward?"

Edward floated out of the pit. A moment later he was standing in front of Ellie.

"I found this when I was eight," he said. "Of course, the tunnel's much older than the folly. Someone was clever enough to link the two together. Oh, don't look so surprised. You knew about the priest's hole, and the hidden chamber. It all just goes a bit further… Here, I say, get off!" He backed away as Ellie tried to hug him. "You know that doesn't work, anyway."

"I thought…" Ellie caught her breath. "I thought you were…"

"If you say "dead"," Edward told her. "I'll pull your hair again. You didn't think I was going to stick around to get toasted like a crumpet on the nursery fire, did you?" His voice softened. "I must say, it's jolly nice to see you."

"Then, what –" Ellie started.

"I managed to slip out of the painting before those idiot yokels from the village picked it up," Edward said. "Been in hiding. I don't know who told them to burn the thing, but someone did. Funny…" He laughed. "We had an old Vicar in the village, who used to talk about one's soul going to the eternal fires. Personally, I thought I was a bit young for that, just yet."

Ellie looked down into the pit. "There's a tunnel from here to the house?"

"'Course," Edward said. "It's delightfully dirty and creepy down there. You'll loathe it."

Ellie stuck her tongue out.

"But first," Edward said. He sat cross-legged on the stone floor of the folly, and Ellie joined him. "Tell me what's been happening."

Ellie had forgotten how much she still had to tell Edward. Her odd dream. The strange journey to the island.

"Postshadowing," Edward said, when Ellie mentioned the other boat. "Echoes of things that happened here. Nothing unusual in that. You could say I'm something of an echo myself." He frowned. "But what was it you saw?"

His expression grew grimmer when Ellie reached the disappearance of Moira.

"I don't like that. If *she*'s started spiriting people away, then she must be getting angry. She was only sent for me."

As always when the governess was mentioned, he fell silent.

Ellie took the words in slowly.

Spiriting away… Sent for me…

She leapt to her feet.

"So that's it! She's come to collect you!"

"It's not *fair*!" Edward burst out. "Why should I have to go, after all this time?"

He sat, with a sulky expression on his face, looking out across the lake.

"Inchwood is my home. I own the place, by rights."

"And this woman… your governess…" Ellie said. "Has come to fetch you?"

"Come to take me away," Edward corrected. "She's what's known as a Spirit Guide. Come to take me to…

oh… I don't know where. When a child dies, they send someone to bear him away." He scowled. "Why did they have to pick that foul old –"

"Edward!" Ellie scolded. "You're a gentleman, remember." She paused. "What's her name?"

Edward hesitated.

"Miss McKendrick. And she was rotten enough when we were alive. Latin verbs. Compound interest sums. Lovely summer days, stuck inside doing French or copper-plate handwriting with her. And then luncheon, or tea. She wouldn't let me have any of the things I liked. Always rice pudding, or prunes…"

He smiled.

"But they got rid of her. In the end."

"Why?" Ellie asked.

"Don't know." Edward shrugged. "Father never told me. She just went away, a few months before… a few months before I did. We'd already been stuck with her for far too long. But Father had to keep her on, after they chucked me out of school – my prep school. I was meant to be going to another school, until…"

He stopped.

"I still don't get it," Ellie said. "I know teaching you can't have been a bundle of joy. But why does she hate you so much?" She paused. "And she still looked young. She must have died young. And why's she only come to get you now? And what's she done to Moira?"

"What is this, a parlour game?" Edward snapped. "How am I meant to know? Oh, come on."

He headed back towards the stone slab.

"Shall we go?"

"Down the tunnel?" Ellie peered over the edge. It seemed a long way down – though there was a ladder, of sorts – iron rungs set into the stone wall inside.

"Unless you can row," Edward said. "It's quicker this way, anyhow."

In three seconds flat, he shot up into the air, and down into the pit.

"Race you!"

"No, Edward!" Ellie shouted. "Hang on!"

There was silence.

Then, slowly, Ellie started to clamber after him.

"It's all right for you," she muttered. "You can't break your neck."

Grimly, Ellie went hand-over-hand, down and down. The rungs were some distance apart and she found it hard making the transition from one to another. She only hoped they were secure.

Eventually, she found herself at the bottom of the dank and grimy pit.

"Come on!" Edward's voice echoed back to her. "This way."

Ellie squinted to make out the long tunnel leading away into the distance. It was so dark…

"Need a little light on a dark subject?" Edward called. His laugh rebounded from the walls. It sounded like the laughter of a giant. "That was one of Father's sayings… Allow me."

A blaze of light filled the tunnel.

"There's no doubt about it," Edward's voice went on. "There are some good points to being a ghost."

Ellie blinked. She followed Edward.

The tunnel seemed to go on for miles, despite Edward saying it was the fastest route. Edward drifted along with no effort at all. Ellie cast a glare in his direction every time she had to pause for breath.

She didn't know how far underground they were, but they must have reached quite a depth. It was cold and damp and she could tell she was the first person to use this route in a very long time.

The first living person, at least.

"Did you used to play down here?" Ellie asked.

"Yes," Edward said. "And it was a splendid hiding place. Strange, isn't it?" He smiled. "I was hiding from her then, too."

They rounded a bend.

"Once, I was down here a whole night," he went on. "When they found I was missing in the morning, there was the most frightful fuss."

"Hey!" Ellie's eyes widened. "That's a point. What must Mum be thinking? She'll be going ballistic. Totally."

"Totally…ballistic…" Edward shook his head. "It's worse than learning Latin with you, sometimes. What *language* do you people speak?"

Ellie ignored him.

"Why did you come down here, that time? Was that Miss McKendrick, too?"

"Well…." Edward muttered. "I only put a centipede

in her bed." He sniggered. "Father was furious, when she told him."

"You want to be careful," Ellie said. "In that dream I told you about, she had this huge book. She's written down all the bad things you've done. It looks like you're in a lot of trouble, once she gets hold of you."

"That's what we're trying to prevent," Edward said. "Remember?"

They turned another corner. They seemed to be going upward.

"What about your father, Ellie?" asked Edward. "Is he away on business?"

"No." Ellie looked at the damp and dirty ground. "He just doesn't live with us. At the moment. That's all." She looked back at Edward. "They're still married, my Mum and Dad. They're not divorced."

"I should think not, indeed!" Edward looked shocked. "Father knew a chap, got divorced. He was never invited to dinner again. Had to resign from all his clubs." He paused. "You don't see your father now, then?"

"At weekends…" Ellie said. "Sometimes. And he's coming here, tomorrow." A thought occurred to her. "Of course, you couldn't know what it's like, not to have your parents around."

Edward laughed.

"I hardly knew when they were. Do you know how much time I spent with them, usually? One hour a day. New collar on, and best behaviour. The rest of the time I was stuck upstairs in the nursery, with nannies, or rotten old Miss Mc when I was older. The footmen brought me my meals on a tray." He frowned. "If I had gone away again, to school… Father was talking about my spending the holidays there. I shouldn't have seen him, or Mother, even when term was over."

There was a new source of light ahead of them.

"Welcome to my parlour." Edward grinned. "You're the first mortal being in decades to enter the hidden chamber."

Ellie found herself standing in a large, stone room. There were ridges all the way around the walls, like shelves. A long, stone outcrop from the left-hand wall could have served as a bed or as a table.

"You'd be surprised how many of my ancestors hid out, here," Edward told her. "Hiding away from Civil Wars and what have you." He smiled slightly. "Well, we were never that keen on fighting."

He drifted over to the shelves.

"And in later years, I often came here myself. I had quite a nice little den."

Ellie could see things on the shelves now – old and tattered books – the sticky remains of a bottle of lemonade – and a faded and dirty chocolate box. She shuddered to think what might be living in there.

"Sorry I can't offer you anything," Edward said. "I had a jolly good stock of tuck here, once."

He sat on the stone outcrop and Ellie joined him.

"What can have happened to Moira?" Ellie said. "She was acting weird. Could Miss McKendrick have done something to her mind?"

"Shouldn't be at all surprised," Edward said. "She was always doing things to mine. She wouldn't let me have *any* cake at all, one tea-time, until I'd recited the twelve times table backwards, three times."

"What's eleven times twelve?" Ellie asked.

Edward made no reply.

"Ssh!" Ellie said. "Listen!"

Somewhere nearby, they could hear voices.

"Someone can't just disappear from an island, without a boat."

"Probably playing some prank again." Ellie couldn't mistake Charlie's voice. "I told you she was behaving weirdly."

"It's Mum!" Ellie hissed. "And Charlie!"

The voices drew nearer.

"Well, *I'm* not getting wet through again," Charlie's voice whined on. "I suggest you call the police, right now."

"I think that might be the best thing to do, Marcus," Mum's voice said.

Ellie looked at her watch. She leapt up.

"It's five o'clock! I've been away for, like… *hours*!"

"Ah, well," said Edward. "They do say absence makes the heart grow fonder."

Ellie looked around. "Where are we? How d'you get out of here?"

Edward pointed to the wall in front of them.

"Over there. There's a little family crest – how's that for style? You press it, and a door opens."

He grinned.

"This used to be me. Sitting here, hearing voices, once they'd worked out where I was. And wondering how I was going to talk my way out of trouble."

"In that case," Ellie said. "You'd better think how *I'm* going to."

She turned.

"Edward? Edward!"

An empty stone seat met her eyes.

"Oh, no!" Ellie howled. "Don't you dare! You're not doing that to me again –"

Silence.

Ellie took a deep breath.

Then she moved to find the hidden door.

"I have to say, Judith," said Marcus, "that your first few days here have not been entirely consistent with what we look for at Journeyback."

He strutted around the Manor's library.

"Let's review your progress, shall we? Second day – guests' possessions go missing from an important event. Third day – your daughter goes off on a pleasure trip to the island, before disappearing. We now have to call in police – which is the last thing we need. Now, I'm not saying you're responsible for everything that's gone wrong –"

"Thanks," muttered Mum, as she stood on the hearthrug. "That's good of you."

"But as an Events Organiser," Marcus concluded, "you seem, shall we say, rather neglectful of our public image."

He reached out to rest his hand against a shelf of leather-bound books.

The next moment, the shelf wasn't there.

Mum stared as the whole section of bookshelves slid aside, sending Marcus crashing into the dark space beyond.

A doorway was revealed.

"Oh…" said Ellie. "Sorry… Hi."

Chapter Twelve

"Get in there!" Mum ushered Ellie into the flat. "Go straight to your room! And stay there 'til I tell you to come out! You can consider yourself grounded!"

She followed Ellie into her room.

"This really is the limit, Ellie. When I give you and Charlie freedom to lead your own lives, I don't expect that freedom to be abused. It was ridiculous, and foolhardy, at your age, to explore those tunnels. Let alone going off on your own in a boat!"

Ellie stared at her mother. "But – I wasn't on my own. Moira was in the boat with me –"

"That's *enough*!" Mum shouted. "I don't want to hear lies, on top of everything else! How *could* she have been with you, when she was with us? Charlie and I took our eyes off you–"

Ellie noticed Mum didn't mention being asleep.

"– for no more than a few minutes, max," Mum went on. "At the end of which time Moira came and told us where you were."

"Where's Moira now?" Ellie asked.

"She's gone home," Mum answered. "Won't be back 'til Monday. Not that I'm involving her in this, any more. You've caused me enough professional embarrassment as it is. Honestly, this is meant to be my day off!"

She sank onto Ellie's bed.

"In the meantime," she said. "Charlie had to get out the inflatable dinghy he uses on summer camp, and go out with one of the volunteers to look for you. It's not far, but it was far enough. When they found the boat abandoned, and you gone…"

She closed her eyes.

"Halfway back, they started shipping water. It's a good job that volunteer had his Lifesaving badge."

"Mum," Ellie said. "I'm sorry. But I promise you, I wasn't on my own. Moira was with me. At least, going out."

"And how did she get back to us so quickly?" Mum demanded. "And without the boat? Did she fly?"

Ellie fell silent.

"I don't know," Mum said, "why you persist in telling me these lies. Honestly, Ellie, I'm starting to wonder if I can believe anything you tell me. This is the worst day we've had since your Dad left."

Ellie was surprised. Mum had never said anything like that before.

"I suggest you go to bed," Mum finished. "Right now. I'll bring you some tea, or something, in a bit… oh, just go to bed. I've done with you."

She made her exit.

"The rest of the house is out of bounds to you, until I tell you otherwise. And that includes those tunnels."

She banged the door shut.

Ellie decided to do as she was told. She got into bed – fully clothed – and pulled the covers right up to her. After exploring the cold, dark tunnels, it felt surprisingly good.

What *was* happening? Why was Moira lying? And how could Mum have seen Moira, when Moira had been with Ellie?

It all felt too much for her, all of a sudden. She sank back onto the pillow, trying to forget Edward and Moira and ghosts and tunnels and things that had happened far, far too long ago…

Ellie sat up abruptly in bed.

She hadn't actually meant to sleep. But it seemed she had.

Now, she was awake again. And it was dark.

She knew straight away that something was wrong. The flat was silent. Even at night, she could hear the fridge humming in the kitchen, or Charlie's snoring. She could hear nothing. The place was like –

Like the grave.

A smile crossed Ellie's face. This sort of thing didn't scare her any more. She was used to it now.

She glanced at her watch. Five minutes to twelve.

There wasn't long to wait.

She sat, hands folded in front of her. Somehow, she knew what to expect.

Sure enough, five minutes later the clock in the next room began to strike midnight. On the final stroke, her door started to swing open.

And Miss McKendrick stepped into the room.

"There you are," Ellie said. She looked at her watch again. "You're fifteen seconds late." She remembered Edward's words of earlier. "What kept you?"

"You really are the most insolent little girl." Miss McKendrick came and stood by Ellie's bed. "And despite my earlier warning, you persist in interfering."

"It was you, wasn't it?" Ellie asked. "You transported Moira away from the island. And what about that mist? Did you want to strand me out there? Or just make it look like people couldn't trust me? You didn't want anyone messing up your plans for Edward, did you? I've found out too much."

"Too much?" The governess smiled. "My dear, you know nothing."

Her voice softened a little.

"Whatever you may think of me, my work was to take care of children. I wish you no harm. Very soon, Edward and I will be gone. And you will continue with your life. Until the time comes for one of my associates to pass final judgment on you."

She met Ellie's eye.

"Though I would advise you not to bring that date forward."

"Edward belongs here," Ellie said. "And I'm not going to let you take him away."

She stared right into Miss McKendrick's eyes.

"I'm not frightened of you."

Miss McKendrick vanished.

Without a flicker of fear, Ellie turned to see the

governess standing on the other side of the bed.

"And you can forget all that stuff. Even Edward can do that one. I've seen it all, now."

"How brave you are," Miss McKendrick said. "Clearly I underestimated you."

She took a step closer to Ellie.

"You are determined to persist with your actions? There is no way I can prevail upon you to change your mind?"

"I told you," Ellie said. "Edward's my friend. I'm going to help him. And nothing you can do will frighten me off."

Miss McKendrick stepped away from the bed.

"I see."

From nowhere, she produced a massive book similar to the one Ellie had seen before.

"You may not be aware, but a considerable amount of information has already been recorded on you. As with every living being. I know everything about you. I know where you attended school, the names of your friends. The illnesses that you've suffered. The good things you've done. And the bad."

She opened the book, and glanced down a page.

"I even know your nightmares."

She smiled.

"I see that when you were six years old, you attended a school fair. And someone was giving you a glimpse of the animal kingdom. Specifically, snakes."

She looked up from the book.

"And you didn't like snakes, did you? The way they…

slithered. The way they looked cold, and slimy. And were watching you. Ready to lunge. Ready to bite…"

She held out a hand towards Ellie's bed.

"And for months afterwards, you lay and read until after midnight. Forced yourself to stay awake. Because you knew that as soon as you fell asleep…"

Ellie sat, motionless.

She didn't dare to look left, or right.

Because she could hear hissing.

And she knew what she would see.

"I'm not frightened," she repeated loudly. "They're nightmares. They're not real."

"Real enough to you when you were six," Miss McKendrick said. "Don't you understand? All those fears, the nightmares that lie buried forever within your mind. I have the power to make them come true."

The hissing grew louder. And Ellie was no longer able to look away.

From the base of the bed, six small, green heads appeared, fixing their hypnotic gaze on Ellie. Six long, green bodies followed, emerging as one from the mattress where they had made their nest.

Ellie shrank back into bed as the six snakes slithered across her, their eyes taunting her as they prepared to bite.

"I'm *not* afraid!" Ellie cried. But the pitch of her voice seemed to have gone up. She sounded much younger – and much less sure. "What do you really want with Edward?"

"Stay away from matters you don't understand,

Eleanor," Miss McKendrick said. "This is your final warning. I wish you no harm, as I said before. But Edward is now my property. He'll be gone from here before another night has passed."

Ellie flinched. One of the snakes had its head right up to her neck. But still she battled on.

"No – no!"

"Shall we try another nightmare?" Miss McKendrick's voice grew louder, as if amplified from every corner of the room. "The one you had in hospital? The one where the walls were closing in to crush you? Or what about the one after the burglary, where there was someone in the house again… and this time, he had a gun…"

Ellie could feel it all – she could sense the gunman in the room – knew the walls were coming in towards her – and the snake was opening its mouth –

"A last warning, Eleanor!" Miss McKendrick bellowed. "Leave Master Edward to me!"

"I won't!" Ellie screamed.

The forked tongue of the snake was brushing her cheek.

"*I won't!*"

Ellie sat up abruptly in bed.

She was breathing very fast. And the sweat was running down her face. Her clothes were soaked.

It was daylight.

Very carefully, she looked around the room, then down at the bed. She moved her hand very slowly to feel the edge of the mattress.

She flinched as someone hammered on the door.

"Ellie! Can I come in?"

Ellie caught her breath. "Yeah?"

Charlie opened the door and entered.

"Hello, small person." There was a smirk hovering around his lips. "Mum wants you. You're still confined to the flat, though. She says you're to come and eat. You were already asleep when she came in last night."

He gave her a sour look.

"Cheers for the swim yesterday."

He noted Ellie's appearance.

"Euww. You look nice. Sleeping in your clothes now? I'll go and turn the shower on."

Ellie remained in bed a moment longer, staring at the spot where Miss McKendrick had stood.

Chapter Thirteen

Saturday morning was dull and cloudy. Ellie could hear rain tapping at the tiny windows of their flat.

She ate her cereal and toast in silence. Charlie was texting. Mum was looking at paperwork, and said nothing. Ellie was left in no doubt that she was still in disgrace.

First thing after breakfast, Ellie sat with her sketchbook, drawing furiously. Snakes appeared. Then the man with the gun.

As soon as she had drawn the pictures, she ripped them out of the book and tore them into fragments, the smallest she could manage, before crumpling all of them into one lump of waste paper.

Once Mum and Charlie had left for the Site Office, Ellie put her easel up. She set to work at a ferocious speed on a painting of Inchwood Manor. The outline appeared, then the timbers. By noon, the hydrangeas had been added, and the rose-trees that grew near the edge of the lawn...

"Boo!"

Ellie jumped, and smeared red paint right across the picture.

"Edward –!"

"Edward?" A familiar voice sounded puzzled. "My name's Jon. Last time I looked."

Ellie turned.

"Dad!"

For a moment, she forgot everything, her painting, Miss McKendrick, Edward. She might have been that six-year-old again as she ran to hug her father.

Dad grinned. "Who's Edward, then? Got a boyfriend now? Hope he's rich."

"Just a friend," Ellie said.

"Oh." Dad noted the damage to the picture. "Sorry." He took a closer look. "And how's my talented girl? Another masterpiece coming up."

"We're doing OK," Ellie said.

She really wanted to tell Dad everything… all the things that had happened the last few days. But how?

"Where is everyone?" Dad helped himself to an apple from the bowl of fruit on the table. "Where's your mother, and Charlie?" He sat down and put his feet up on the tabletop. "Some fella in a high-powered suit showed me in. Gave me a right snooty look."

"That's Marcus," Ellie said.

She was already smiling. It was impossible to take anything seriously when Dad was around. Even the sight of him made her feel better. While Mum and Charlie were all work and responsibility, Dad was always looking for fun, thinking up the next game, planning the next party… or outing… or birthday surprise…

Dad put the half-eaten apple down on the table and

started to make another raid on the fruit bowl.

"Hey!" Ellie made a grab for his hands. "You'll spoil your lunch!" She started to laugh as Dad picked out two oranges and started to juggle them. "Hey, don't muck about –"

The green baize door opened. Mum stood there.

An orange hit the floor.

"Oh," Dad said. "Hi."

"Made yourself at home, I see," Mum said. "You're early. But no matter. I've got a meeting at two, anyway. And they're putting a new fire alarm in, I've got to supervise. The meal's going to be cut short, I'm afraid."

Dad stood up.

"Nothing changes, does it?" He turned to Ellie. "The sun's coming out. Are you going to show me some of this great estate, then, while your mother cooks the lunch? I always knew you'd end up lady of the manor somewhere."

"Yeah, sure." Ellie moved to find her fleece. "I can show you the rose garden… maybe the lake…"

"She *was* grounded," Mum put in.

"Well, I've just un-grounded her," Dad answered. "I'm only here for a few hours. 'Least you can do is let Ellie show me round."

He headed for the door.

"Lunch at one, was it?"

After a brief hesitation, Ellie followed him.

She left the flat to the sound of Mum crashing about among pots and pans.

The sun was just breaking through the clouds as Ellie and her father crunched their way across the gravel path towards the lawns.

Dad looked back at the house.

"You've really got this place spot-on, in that painting," he said. "You've even caught the way the sunlight shines off those windows."

He paused.

"Are you happy here, Ellie?"

Ellie shrugged.

"Yeah."

"We're a long way from our old lives, aren't we?" Dad said. "Remember? – I used to pick you up in the car after Book Club? Then there was Charlie's football team… I don't think he ever plays now, does he?"

Ellie smiled.

"He's not a footballer, any more. He's an "entrepreneur". Suits, ties, meetings, mobiles. Going to make us all millionaires."

"I suppose he knows what he's doing." Dad caught Ellie's eye. "Try and remember something for me, will you?" He gave the front windows of the house another glance. "Don't forget about the sunlight."

Ellie shook her head.

"Where's this lake, then?" Dad went on. "Should have told me. I'd have brought the yacht. Unfortunately, I lent it to the supermodel next door, you know, so I'm having to make do with a toy boat 'til the butler gets back from his holiday."

As ever, Ellie laughed.

They stayed out for ages. Ellie showed Dad the lake and told him about the island and the folly. They went on to the rear lawn, then walked beneath the chestnut trees.

By the time they returned to the house, they were half an hour late for lunch.

Ellie picked at her food.

She wasn't enjoying the meal. Mum's lamb chops had practically had to be scraped off the pan, yet the courgettes in her ratatouille were still rock hard.

Ellie had expected it to be fun. The family, together again.

Everyone was eating in silence.

Finally, Dad spoke.

"When do you two start school, then?"

"Next week," Charlie answered. "Pleased to see they've got schools out here, at least. This is an important year for me. I'm carrying on with Business Studies. And Information Systems."

Ellie looked down at her plate.

"I'm hoping my school's got a Book Club."

"You've got terrific surroundings here, anyway," Dad said. "And I hear you're already making yourselves useful around the house. When the guidebook comes out you can autograph one for me, Ellie."

"We should get together more often," Ellie said. "For meals… picnics…"

She avoided Mum's eye. She addressed her father.

"You could come down every weekend, in the summertime."

"I'd rather come to you, Dad," Charlie put in. "I could come up to London at weekends, maybe." He drained his glass of water. "I mean, after the divorce."

There was a sudden, terrible silence.

Charlie met his parents' gaze. Then he looked at Ellie.

"You mean – you still haven't –"

Ellie looked from one parent to the other.

"Ellie…" Mum said. "We were going to tell you. Before we left London. But we all thought it might be better to let you get settled, before –"

Ellie flung her plate aside and ran from the room.

Ellie refused to leave her bedroom for the remainder of Dad's visit. She continued with her painting of the Manor, slapping on every last drop of grey and black, making the sky darker and stormier.

Eventually, Dad tapped at the door, entered. He'd brought an apology, of some kind. Words floated over her head… *sometimes, when two people… still be a family… just want you to be happy…*

She couldn't take them in.

When the time came to see Dad off, she could barely look at him, or at Mum. When she stood in an awkward family group of three to wave to him, and she saw his battered white car disappear down the drive, she could have cried.

It felt like forever.

She did little for the rest of the day. She stayed in her

room, painted a bit more. When teatime came she told Mum she wasn't hungry.

She went to bed early. There didn't seem to be much to stay up for.

She wasn't afraid of bed, or the snakes, now. They didn't matter any more.

As she finally started to drift off, she suddenly remembered what Miss McKendrick had said about Edward.

He'll be gone from here before another night has passed.

The bedroom light flicked on.

Ellie woke up, blearily.

"Ellie?" A woman's voice spoke. "Are you all right?"

Ellie focused.

"Moira? What are you doing here?"

"Working late," Moira answered. She came and sat on the edge of Ellie's bed. "I had to come and see you before I left."

Ellie sat up.

"I thought you weren't coming today. What happened to you? On the island?" She frowned. "And why did you lie? Mum said –"

"I'm sorry about that." Moira's voice was low and urgent. "But I had to put them off the scent, for a while. Ellie, I've discovered something. About what really happened here. And I need your help."

Ellie blinked.

"How do you know what's been happening here?"

"Keeping my eyes open," Moira answered. "Looking into things. You've been led astray, Ellie. Everyone's been deceiving you. Including Marcus."

Ellie's eyes grew.

"Marcus?"

Moira nodded.

"Remember the portrait? But I know what he's up to, now. I know how I was transported off the island – and why. The answer lies in the tunnels."

She stood up.

"Come with me."

Ellie rose. She put her fleece and her trainers on.

"Where are we going?"

Very quietly, Moira led Ellie out of her room and across the living room. The clock on the wall said eleven-thirty. Charlie and Mum had gone to bed.

They stepped out of the flat.

Ellie followed Moira along the hall and past the door to the cellar. They turned into a corridor that led to the dining room and billiard room.

"What's going on, Moira?" she whispered.

In answer, Moira turned to one of the panelled walls. She ran her fingers along the rim of the top section of panelling.

There was a grating, grinding sound as the whole section of wall slid aside.

Ellie looked into the space beyond. The panels had hidden an ancient stone wall – and set into the wall, below floor level, was a large, rectangular hole.

"The priest's hole," Moira said. "That's where the answer is."

She held out her hand to Ellie.

"Come on, then."

Ellie stared.

"Down there?"

"If you want to know what's going on," Moira said. "Come on. I'll give you a hand."

Bewildered, Ellie stepped to the edge and took Moira's hand.

There were steps there, of a sort, but they were very uneven, and Ellie found it difficult to keep her balance.

She caught her breath.

"Moira…" She struggled to hold on. "What's happening?"

Very slowly, a smile crossed Moira's face.

"I told you I'd found the answer."

She let go.

Ellie screamed as she fell six feet into the hole.

She made a hard landing. Pain tore through her ankle as her leg twisted under her.

Moira appeared, silhouetted in the doorway above.

"Don't bother to scream. The priest's hole was designed for secrecy. You could be down there for months. And no one would know."

Ellie found tears springing to her eyes.

"Why? *Why?*"

Moira stood a moment, looking down at Ellie.

"I warned you not to interfere."

There was a blaze of light. Moira shimmered – and transformed.

A tall, forbidding figure in blouse and skirt appeared, carrying a cane.

Miss McKendrick smiled.

"I told you I'd be watching you."

Chapter Fourteen

Ellie stared at Miss McKendrick through the tears.

"Then Moira –"

"Never existed," Miss McKendrick said. "I based her on those ridiculous people who came to look around. And I heard plenty of college stories here, in the old days."

She smiled.

"I came to you, just when you needed a friend."

"So that's how you got off the island!" Ellie paused. "It was you who told them to burn Edward in that portrait too, wasn't it? You used Moira for that. What were you trying to do? Scare him out of hiding?"

Miss McKendrick's voice hardened.

"You were warned, Eleanor. Once. Twice. Now, Edward is coming away with me. Tonight. And this house will go to its doom."

She extended a hand towards the panelled wall.

"I'm so sorry that you and your family shan't be here to see it."

Her grim smile was the last thing Ellie saw before the panel slammed shut.

The narrow space of the priest's hole was plunged into darkness.

Ellie was too stunned to do anything for several moments, even to notice how dark it was, or how little air there was, or how much her ankle hurt.

She felt in the pocket of her fleece and found her phone. She switched it on, creating a dim, bluish light that barely showed the tiny stone chamber around her.

There was no signal.

A memory was coming back… the island… and Moira's reaction to being photographed. Quickly, she opened the gallery on her phone, found the images she'd taken of them at the folly.

Each of the pictures showed Ellie. And next to her was an empty space.

Ellie let her head drop. Then she let the tears come, properly now, hours of worry about Mum and Dad and Edward gushing out of her.

"Oh, crikey," moaned a voice. "Not the waterworks, please! I never could stand to see a girl cry. I had a cousin, used to howl if you so much as looked at her, or took one of her sweets…"

"Edward." Ellie was too weary even to be surprised.

"I say." Edward appeared, squashed into the space beside her. "That's a bit of a turn up for the books, isn't it? Miss Goody-Two-Shoes Secretary being old Miss Mc."

"Did you hear everything she said?" Ellie asked.

Edward nodded.

"Going to take me away, tonight." He paused. "So, what's the plan?"

"Plan?" Ellie yelled. "Edward! We're trapped underground!"

"Trapped, you think?" Edward smiled. "I wouldn't have said that. This is part of the tunnels, remember? Priests did need an escape route occasionally."

He pointed to his left. Ellie could just make out a series of footholds set into the wall.

"There's a tunnel entrance just above us. We're not far from the centre of the network. There's an exit into the morning room, and stairs leading up... Come along."

Ellie struggled to move.

"My ankle..."

"Oh, good grief." Edward rolled his eyes. "Hang on. There's a trick I've always wanted to try. Never had the chance, 'til now."

He held out his right hand to Ellie.

It became solid.

"Can't do this for long," he said. "Not like old Miss McKendrick. She fooled you completely. Solid human being... You'd better get a move on."

Ellie gave him a look of wonder as she took his hand.

With Edward's help, she scrambled upward and into the tunnel. Edward gave her a smile that was almost gentlemanly.

"At last, after reading all those tales of knights and dragons. A real damsel in distress."

The tunnel was much narrower than those they'd explored earlier. Led by Edward, they advanced towards a doorway that was gradually becoming visible in the distance.

"That's the morning room exit," Edward said. He sounded proud. "Not bad, eh?"

"No," Ellie admitted. "Now, maybe you can think up what we're going to do next."

She paused.

There was a faint sound…gentle… rippling…

She and Edward looked down to see water running around their feet. They looked back.

It was coming from the tunnel.

"What –?" Edward looked dumbfounded. "What's happening? Has someone let the bath overflow?"

Ellie blinked.

"The lake…"

She looked at Edward.

"Don't you get it? These tunnels reach right to the lake. If the lake floods… and the entrance to the tunnels there is open…"

"But how could…?" Edward started.

His eyes met Ellie's.

"Miss McKendrick!"

"Has she got the power to make a flood?" Ellie asked. "To raise the water level of the lake?"

Edward frowned.

"Unfortunately, yes. She's a Spirit Guide, they're very powerful. They have power over all the elements – earth, wind, fire…"

He looked at the pool. It was deepening.

"And water."

Ellie remembered Miss McKendrick's words.

This house will go to its doom.

She grasped Edward's hand.

"Come on."

Pursued by the sound of water, they ran. The sound was no longer that of a trickle, but of a rushing torrent.

Ellie remembered something else Miss McKendrick had said.

You and your family shan't be here.

"Mum…" she muttered. "And Charlie…"

Her face set in a frown.

"We'd better get out of here. And above ground. Now." She looked around. "Stairs, you said – where are they?"

Edward moved forward.

"This way."

A sub-tunnel off to the right led to a set of ancient stone steps. Ellie followed Edward up, and up, and up. Every step she climbed made her wince with pain from her ankle. She had counted thirty steps – and thirty stabs of pain – before they'd even reached the top.

"You certainly make a fellow work," Edward said. He grimaced as Ellie gripped his hand more tightly.

The stone staircase led to an archway that was covered in mould and cobwebs. Ellie spluttered, and Edward did his best to repress a grin, as a spider's web brushed across her face.

"Where does this come out?" Ellie gasped.

Edward smiled.

"I think you'll recognise it."

A panelled door slid aside. Ellie stepped through.

She found herself staring into the eyes of Edward's tin soldiers.

"The nursery!"

Edward released Ellie, reached above them and pressed. The panel slid shut, blocking out the distant sound of water.

They moved into the centre of the room. As always, the toys looked abandoned and eerie in the semi-darkness.

"Welcome home!" Edward crowed. "Who's for lemonade? Then perhaps a few songs on the jolly old piano! Take me away from my home, would she? I soon showed her…"

"Edward," said Ellie very slowly.

"Teach her to tangle with a Fitzberranger." Edward aimed a few mock-punches at an imaginary opponent.

"Edward!" said Ellie more loudly.

The electric light flicked on, all by itself. Edward turned.

Standing next to the bookshelves was Miss McKendrick.

"I really must congratulate you," she said to Ellie. "But then, I didn't really expect you to stay there to drown."

She reached out a hand towards Edward.

"Thank you for bringing him to me."

"You leave him –" Ellie started forward.

Miss McKendrick flung out her other hand. A vortex of light spun out of nowhere, a network of light-beams imprisoning Ellie.

Ellie screamed.

"Don't you dare –" Edward started, but his voice was high-pitched and timid.

"Oh, be quiet!" Miss McKendrick glared. "Master Edward, you've behaved very badly. And it's time for you to pay the penalty for your actions."

She reached out again towards him.

"Come with me."

She looked back at Ellie.

"If you want your little friend to survive. What shall it be this time, Eleanor? The snakes? The hospital? It's amazing what can be done with the power of the mind."

She took a step closer to Ellie.

"Or shall I simply increase the fear? Until your nervous system collapses, and your mind burns out? Or I could send you to sleep, like I did your family, by the lake. But this time, there would be no waking." She turned to Edward. "The decision is yours."

Edward looked at the floor.

"What's this *really* about?" Ellie shouted. "Why have you got it in for Edward?"

For a moment, she thought she saw a flicker of pain cross Miss McKendrick's face. But then it was gone.

Miss McKendrick pointed towards the far wall.

A section of panelling slid open. Ellie managed to turn her head to see. It looked like the other tunnel entrances… with a black space beyond… but there was something different about it. It looked transparent, shimmering, like Edward… unreal…

Miss McKendrick moved to Edward.

"Come."

Edward gave Ellie a last, helpless look.

Then he took Miss McKendrick's hand.

Miss McKendrick led Edward towards the black space.

"I suggest you forget you ever saw this, Eleanor. I'm still prepared to be merciful. You'll be released. I advise you to go. And leave this sad place behind."

Ellie struggled and yelled.

The panel slid shut, and Ellie was left alone.

At once, the light-beams disappeared. Ellie fell forward and straight onto the train set. She felt the station and signal box crunch under her.

Bruised, exhausted, she lay upon the broken toys.

As soon as she could move, she hobbled across to the panelling and searched for the entrance, any hidden controls.

There was nothing. Somehow, she knew that hadn't been a real door.

For a moment, she stood staring at the wall. Another tear came to her eye. She brushed it away.

There was nothing she could do for Edward now. Right now, her job was to get downstairs, and warn Mum about the flood.

She paused. She looked back at where she had fallen.

Something had happened to the train set table. She remembered hearing a clicking sound as she fell.

A drawer had sprung out from the edge of the

table. A drawer that previously hadn't been visible.

Ellie looked inside.

The drawer was packed with items. Papers, mostly, old and brown around the edges, their ink faded with age. But also books. Notebooks, bound in leather. There were other items too. A very old sepia photograph of a middle-aged woman, stern-faced and unsmiling. A silver inkwell. A locket, marked with the letter E, on a slender, gold chain. Ellie opened the locket. It contained a picture of a young man with long, dark hair and a beard.

Ellie knew him straight away. It was the man she'd seen on the lake. And the woman in the boat with him, laughing and happy, had been Miss McKendrick.

Very carefully, Ellie picked out an envelope. It was open. A few flakes of sealing-wax tumbled back into the drawer.

The envelope was addressed to *Miss E. McKendrick*, with the Manor's address beneath.

After a pause, Ellie reached inside. Not for the first time since coming to Inchwood, she had the feeling that she was trespassing.

The envelope contained not one, but three folded letters. She unfolded the first one. It was only a page in length. She squinted to read the spidery scrawl.

Dear Emily

I apologise for the shortness of this note, but I must ask you not to communicate with me again. You must see that the situation has become impossible, and that any friendship we might once have enjoyed can no longer continue. I am returning herewith your last letter, and also send a letter I have received from Mr Fitzberranger, which I hope makes everything plain. By now he may already have acted in accordance with it. I sent warning as early as I possibly could.

Please accept my very best wishes for your future.

Kind regards
Mortimer Harvey

Ellie turned to the second letter. It was written in stout, sloping handwriting, different from the first. The opening lines had been written so hurriedly she couldn't read them. Then:

…and I feel so miserable, when you have to be away. Edward was so horrid today, and every moment I was thinking of you. I keep remembering that first time we met. As soon as I saw you, it was as though my concerns just vanished – my mother's illness, my schooling going to waste, and the fact that Edward is utterly un-teachable. None of it mattered any more, because I'd found you. It was amusing at first, having to conceal everything from the family, for I knew what they thought of me! I've heard the murmurs, in the drawing room! Poor little thing, with her books, and what of her father? – left when she was a child – he was something in Trade, you know! But then, no one ever expects a governess to have feelings.

Mortimer, why cannot we tell them now? Why must we continue this pretence? I know you do not love her, and you cannot mean to marry her simply for her wealth? I'm sure Mr Fitzberranger is beginning to suspect. He is determined that nothing should stand in the way of the engagement, and Miss Sally's happiness. You must…

Ellie opened the third letter. It was written in yet another hand.

… clearly, Mortimer, the matter must be resolved with as little scandal as possible, in order to preserve Sally's reputation, and that of our family. There is no alternative. The young woman must be made to understand that she must go, and Edward will be sent away again to school. In a situation such as this, she can scarcely expect more than one week's notice, or anything in terms of a reference. I think you should not visit us until after her departure.

I have spoken to Sally, and she is sensible and practicable enough to offer you forgiveness. I sincerely hope, Mortimer, that your married life will bring less unpleasantness to this household than the events which have gone before.

Yours, etc…

Ellie squinted to read the signature.

C.G. Fitzberranger.

Was that Edward's father?

She knew she had very little time. She tried to piece

together what she'd read with what she had found online.

Her heart was thumping.

Mortimer Harvey. That was the man who had inherited the estate from Edward's father. And… wasn't Sally short for Sarah? That was Edward's sister. Mortimer Harvey's wife. They were the ancestors of the Miss Harvey who'd passed the Manor to Journeyback.

And the "young woman" who had come between Mortimer and Sally, at the time they were engaged… was Miss McKendrick…

Quickly, Ellie made for the drawer again. She was onto something, at last.

At the very bottom, she could see something gleaming, half-hidden under the other items. She reached beneath and picked out a maroon, leather-backed book with a single word emblazoned in gold lettering.

Journal.

A piece of ribbon bookmarked it at the final entry. The journal stopped suddenly, in the middle of May.

This marks the conclusion of my journal, which ends here with my position in this household, with my reputation – and with my life. I have already written to my Mother, telling her of the circumstances in which I find myself, and saying that I am sorry for bringing our family to further disgrace. I know that, in the absence of my Father, my departure from this Earth will leave her alone in the world, and for that I have expressed my true sorrow.

I keep thinking of those lines from Shakespeare:

> *"There is a tide in the affairs of men*
> *Which, taken at the flood, leads on to fortune…"*

In my case it seems only to have led on to ruin and despair.

As such, I feel it best now to submit myself to the waters. The lake, where Mortimer and I enjoyed such happy times together, shall be my final resting-place.

Ellie's eyes widened.

The bottom of the page was signed.

Emily McKendrick.

She let the book drop to the floor. She was shaking.

"That's why," she whispered. "That's why she hates the family so much. And Edward… Edward's the only one left to remind her of them."

She frowned. But why had Miss McKendrick only come back now? What had changed? She'd only appeared a few days ago… after they'd moved in…and Miss Harvey had moved out.

"Miss Harvey!"

Fighting the pain, Ellie headed for the stairs.

Downstairs, a scene of devastation met her eyes. Water was pouring into the ground floor of the house. A panel was open in the hall, and she guessed the other panels were open in the library, and by the dining room. The water was already a foot deep.

She understood, now, why Miss McKendrick had chosen water as her way of destroying the Manor.

Ellie stood for a moment.

What should she do? She had to get to Miss Harvey – but Mum and Charlie were in the flat, asleep.

She came to a decision.

She waded over to one of Marcus's new fire alarm points, picked up a small, brass ornament from the hall table, and smashed the glass.

An ear-splitting klaxon tore through the Manor.

Ellie had no time to wait to see the result. But she knew that even Charlie wouldn't be able to sleep through that. She could almost hear Mum, taking charge: "Come on! Outside! Now!"

Ellie moved, as quickly as she could, towards the front door.

Forcing herself to ignore her throbbing ankle, her pyjama trousers soaked, Ellie ran into the night.

She hadn't been outside the Manor in darkness before. Her footsteps on the gravel paths sounded louder, and every bush and trailing branch seemed to be a hand put out to bar her way.

By the time she reached the road, she was utterly exhausted, and her ankle hurt like mad. But still she ploughed on, thankful that the village was only half a mile away.

She knew where to find Miss Harvey. Mum had pointed out the cottage when they drove through the village on arrival.

Ellie could only just make out the sign by the door. *Inglenook.*

That was where Miss Harvey was now living with a friend.

Standing on the doorstep, cold, wet, gasping for breath, Ellie pressed the doorbell.

There was no response. Desperately, she rang again and again.

"I hear you!" a sharp voice answered from within. "I hear you. Now, if you boys disturb our peace just once more…"

The door opened. Miss Harvey stood there, in an immaculate dressing-gown, looking annoyed.

Her annoyance vanished as soon as she saw her caller.

"Ellie!"

It was too much for Ellie. She almost fell into the cottage, unable to move another step.

"Dear goodness, what's happened?" Miss Harvey put her thin arms around Ellie's shoulders. "All right, all right, calm yourself. You're here now."

She guided Ellie inside.

Chapter Fifteen

"I'm sorry there's no milk." Miss Harvey passed a mug of tea to Ellie. "My friend was supposed to do the shopping this morning. But she's been called away to the hospital. Her sister had an operation on Friday… I've put plenty of sugar in."

Ellie took the mug gratefully, cradling its warmth in her hands.

"Thank you."

"Now." Miss Harvey took a chair next to Ellie. A warm fire was burning. Ellie had a blanket around her and her trainers were steaming quietly in the hearth. "Tell me everything."

Ellie obeyed. There was so much to tell, and Miss Harvey was the first adult she'd been able to confide in. She held nothing back, no matter how unbelievable it all sounded. Edward… Miss McKendrick and her guise as Moira… the old letters… and the journal.

The more she told, the more she felt relieved. She hadn't realised just how much she'd been bottling up. For the past few days, her only real friend had been a ghost.

Miss Harvey didn't interrupt once. She sat listening intently, every line of her face set in concentration.

When Ellie had no breath left to continue, Miss Harvey rose slowly from her chair.

"I was afraid this would all blow up again. Once I left... I almost told that silly man from Journeyback, then I thought: what's the point? It's all ancient history."

"You know about Miss McKendrick, then?" Ellie asked.

"And what the Fitzberrangers did to her." Miss Harvey went to a tall bookcase that stood near the door. "You know, Ellie, I've never really understood this modern obsession with tracing one's ancestors. They seldom do anything of which one is particularly proud."

With difficulty, she reached for an upper shelf. Ellie moved to help her.

Miss Harvey reached down a large box-file.

"I brought certain things with me. I'd no idea there was so much still at the house."

They went back and sat by the fire. Miss Harvey opened the file. It revealed a store of old documents almost as big as that which Ellie had found.

"I was always aware," Miss Harvey said, "that there had been sightings. Young Edward has been seen by visitors to the house throughout the decades."

She picked out a yellowing newspaper cutting.

Ellie looked at it. It was dated 1976, from a local paper, and the headline read:

Boy's ghost let my tyres down! Is Manor haunted?

Ellie smiled.

"That sounds like him."

"There have been other sightings too," Miss Harvey said. "Nothing confirmed, of course." She passed another cutting. "One as far back as 1938… and here's a letter someone wrote to me after staying in the 1990s…"

"What about Miss McKendrick?" Ellie returned to the question that was filling her mind. "Why has she only just come back now?"

"Miss McKendrick is another story altogether." Miss Harvey reached deeper into the filing box. "There were sightings of her as well, in the early days – after she passed away. A letter here says she was seen outside the housekeeper's room just after Edward's father died in 1910. She was clearly heading for the nursery."

She lifted out a black-bound notebook.

"Then, after Sally and her husband inherited the estate, the situation changed. There have been no further sightings of Miss McKendrick from nineteen hundred and ten until now."

She flicked through several neatly-handwritten pages.

"And this explains why."

Ellie looked.

It was another journal.

November 9ᵗʰ 1910

I cannot speak to Mortimer… he would never believe it, and this whole matter is best closed. But that woman has been seen again! The parlour-maid saw her on the staircase, and was nearly hysterical. I knew that as long as Miss McK. was here… free to roam the house, and the nursery… that my poor dear brother could never rest in peace. And I feared for the welfare of our own child, whose coming is near.

I have taken measures. Mortimer must never know, as he disapproves of spiritualism. Miss Boscoe, my palmist in the village, has an awareness of these matters. And she told me it is possible to create a barrier against such evil spirits. Not exorcism, nothing that need concern the Bishop. In any case, I believe that even the most obnoxious of spirits has the right to a certain freedom.

No, this method is, if you like, the opposite of a curse. A sort of spell that can be used to bring peace and blessing to a house, via one of its occupants. Namely, myself.

I visited Miss Boscoe this afternoon. She is truly an eccentric lady, yet somehow I always feel safe with her. There was a strange aroma as I entered her cottage… incense. On the table were the crystal and the cards. One would hardly think she sings in the choir.

She told me of the risk I would take… the power that would flow through me as keeper of the spell. Such things can have harmful effects… even shorten life. She assured me, however, that our baby would be safe.

I gave my agreement. We chose my symbol of office. Then she held my hands and spoke the words. I have really very little Latin… but it was something about life… and happiness…

and freedom. As she spoke, her eyes were burning… and for a moment, I saw the crystal blaze with light.

I felt quite ordinary, afterwards. And I was back at the Manor long before tea.

Now, it is done. As long as I remain in residence at Inchwood… or those females who come after me… our home shall be free from the influence of Miss McK.

I hope and pray for a daughter.

"There was a daughter," Miss Harvey said. "And later, a son. There have always been female Harveys at Inchwood from then… until now."

She sighed deeply.

"I'm horribly afraid that this is all my fault."

"So that's it!" Ellie cried. "Sally… and all those who came after her… kept Miss McKendrick away. Including you."

She hesitated.

"So what now? We can't ask you to come back. And it's too late, anyway. She's got her revenge. She's got Edward." She frowned. "What did Sally mean – *symbol of office*?"

She looked down at the journal again. At the bottom of the page, Sally had drawn a strange, swirling shape.

Ellie pointed it out.

"Miss Harvey? Do you know what this is?"

"No," Miss Harvey said. "It occurs a few times in

the journal. People of those days used coded symbols in their diaries quite a lot… there's no knowing what they meant."

"No, hang on!" Ellie stared hard at the shape. "I've seen this somewhere before…"

She picked up the journal and rotated it.

"If you turned this picture upside down, and mirrored it…"

She looked at Miss Harvey.

"That's where I saw it! On our first day. Upside down and flipped… it's that pattern on your brooch!"

Miss Harvey stared at the page.

"Good grief."

Ellie was positively dancing with excitement now, her sore ankle almost forgotten.

"Can I see the brooch?"

"It is a family heirloom, of sorts," Miss Harvey said. "Handed down since the nineteenth century. I took it to a dealer once, he told me it was of little value."

Ellie examined the brooch, with its white-embossed design. It was beautifully made. But there didn't seem to be anything unusual about it.

Deflated, she turned back to Miss Harvey.

"So where does that get us?"

"Not very far, I'm afraid." Miss Harvey paused. "Wait a moment. There *is* something else that might relate to this." She rummaged in the filing box. "It's in Sally's journal, but in another volume… the final one. The very last entry, as a matter of fact. Here we are."

She produced another black-bound book and turned to the final page.

Ellie read the entry. Sally must have been unwell when she wrote this. The writing was fainter. Yet the voice of the woman within was as strong as ever.

I know now that my time is near. I have spoken with Miss Boscoe regarding my passing. She tells me that although my life is ebbing to a close, I may still return to conclude what I began… and save my departed brother from her *influence. I leave the custody of Inchwood with my daughter, and then with future daughters … and with the simple trinket they wear to continue my task.*

"That's got to be it!" Ellie said. "She must mean the brooch… the symbol of office… but what does it do?"

"I'm afraid I have no idea." Miss Harvey stood up. "You must get back to the house now. Your mother will be worried… and from what you tell me, there is great danger. Oh." She looked at what Ellie was wearing. "It'll be cold out there… Just a moment."

She left the room.

Ellie picked up the first journal again. The one Sally had been writing when she set up her spell.

What was the point of the brooch? How was it used?

For the first time, her eye was caught by the way the journal entries were written. Many started with an initial letter that was written much larger than the rest, in bright red ink – similar to the way illuminated manuscripts had begun in the Middle Ages.

There were enough letters there to form words in their own right.

Summer is with us again, and the heat has been most oppressive…

By the time Mortimer came down to breakfast…

The cook came to me this afternoon and said…

Ellie grabbed a pad and pen from the little telephone table next to her and flicked through the whole journal, jotting down all the initial letters Sally had highlighted.

S, B, T, T, I, V, L, R, B, E, E, V, A, A, S, O, R, I, I.

She blinked at the pad. Anagrams had never been her strong point.

"These should fit you…" Miss Harvey bustled back into the room, carrying a sweater and a very battered pair of jeans. "Someone brought them for the jumble sale. They should help keep you warm."

"Miss Harvey." Ellie passed the pad and pen over. "Look at these."

Miss Harvey looked. She began copying the letters out again, swapping them around.

"This is where being a crossword fanatic comes into its own. Lib – liberty? Liberation? Oh, of course! I know what this is!"

She scrawled three words rapidly, crossing out the letters above as she did so.

She passed the pad to Ellie.

"*Veritas vos liberabit*. It's Latin. It means: "the truth will set you free"."

"Wow!" Ellie stared at the page. "You're brilliant!"

"Not really," Miss Harvey said. "It's the motto of the Fitzberranger family." She paused. "Ellie… it's written above the entrance to the Manor."

Ellie looked back from the pad to the journal.

"Oh."

Miss Harvey smiled gently.

"I wonder…" she said, "whether it does have any relationship to the brooch. It's a phrase Sally would have known well. And all those who followed her…"

With a burst of strength, Ellie levered herself to her feet.

"I think it *is* time I was getting back. Thanks, Miss Harvey!" She grasped Miss Harvey's hands. "And thanks for the clothes. Mind if I borrow the brooch?"

In less than two minutes, Ellie was out of Miss Harvey's front door, dressed in her fleece over the sweater and jeans, the brooch safely zipped into an inner pocket. She was no longer thinking about the pain that came from walking on her swollen ankle.

"But Ellie," Miss Harvey was still saying, "I really think you should be careful. It could be dangerous…"

Ellie was already halfway up the village street.

Miss Harvey shook her head.

"I only hope those ghosts know what they're in for."

Chapter Sixteen

Ellie stood in the nursery, nervously holding up the brooch.

She was going to feel pretty silly if this didn't work.

Getting back into the house had been near-impossible. The ground floor was now under two feet of water. The fire alarm was still blaring. But there was no sign of anyone.

She had waded across to the door to their flat to check on Mum and Charlie, fighting her way through floating chairs and a sea of Journeyback magazines from the hall table.

The door had refused to open. She knew who was responsible for that. She imagined that Marcus must be trapped in his room too.

She only hoped the heavy old doors would hold the water back as well as they held the occupiers in.

She held the brooch as high as she could. She wished she'd done Latin at school.

"Veritas vos liberabit."

Nothing happened. The only sounds to be heard were the fire alarm along the corridor, and the distant running of water.

She tried again.

"*Veritas. Vos. Liberabit.*"

Nothing.

She caught sight of the portrait hanging on the far wall. The one where Edward had been hiding when Miss McKendrick came.

The young woman in the painting wore a Victorian day-dress and had her golden hair tied back from her face. There was something familiar about the shade of her hair, and those blue eyes. She was wearing a wedding ring. The picture showed her standing by a bookcase, on which Ellie could see several black-bound volumes.

"Of course!" Ellie whispered.

She turned and held the brooch out towards the portrait.

"*Veritas vos liberabit!*"

For a second, nothing happened. Then Ellie stared.

The canvas on which the portrait was painted seemed to be shining. It was no longer a painting, but looked like a window into a room as real as the one in which Ellie stood.

Ellie saw the woman's eyes blink. Her face lost the solemn expression it had worn for the portrait, and softened into a smile.

Then, she took a step forward and reached her hand out of the picture frame.

Ellie realised that the hand was being offered to her. She moved closer and took it. As with Edward, and Moira, it felt just like the hand of a human being. But warmer, and stronger, than Moira's hand had been.

As they grasped hands, the woman moved further forward and out into the nursery. Her long dress drifted behind her as she descended gently to the floor.

Slowly, Ellie released her grasp.

"Hello. Are you Miss Fitzberranger? I mean, Mrs Harvey... Are you Sally?"

The young woman nodded.

"My name is Ellie," Ellie continued. "And... if it's all right... I need your help. Please."

Sally showed no surprise.

"Is it about Edward?" she asked in a gentle voice.

"Yes," Ellie answered. "And Miss McKendrick. She's come back."

For the second time that night, Ellie told her story. Sally took everything in rather faster than Miss Harvey.

"I know where she will have taken him. Into a Psychic Realm... that is, a route to the afterlife. She will pass judgment on him there."

She walked towards the wall where Miss McKendrick had made her exit.

"Come."

She paused, and looked at Ellie's ill-fitting sweater and jeans.

"I think perhaps something a little more... ladylike."

She made a movement with her hand. Ellie looked down to see the clothes she was wearing shimmer, soften and change colour.

She found herself wearing a Victorian girl's dress in pale pink.

Sally took Ellie's hand again.

"Come with me. And don't be afraid."

They stepped forward and straight through the panelled wall.

Ellie blinked.

They seemed to be back in the nursery. Yet the room was different. She couldn't hear the flood or the fire alarm. The faces on the soldiers looked more sinister. Everything was a little darker.

"We are no longer in the house," Sally said. "This is Miss McKendrick's Realm. This is where you saw her before. It's an echo of the real Inchwood. A copy she created for herself within the spirit world."

She opened the nursery door. Ellie followed.

"Where will she be?"

"Somewhere deep, and secluded." Sally paused and concentrated. "Somewhere close to the epicentre, where this and all other worlds meet. She's trying to screen herself… but I can sense Edward. We must go down …"

She glided across the corridor.

"The cellar."

They started to descend the stairs to the ground floor.

"Welcome!"

Ellie jumped as the voice of Miss McKendrick boomed out from nowhere.

"Welcome, Miss Sally. And Eleanor. I must congratulate you both. You have seen the fate of the house. Now you've arrived just in time to see that of Master Edward."

"Miss McKendrick." Sally spoke calmly, but firmly. "You have misused your position as a Spirit Guide. You no longer have the authority to pass judgment on the departed."

"You seem to be showing a sudden interest in me, Miss Sally." The voice sounded amused. "If only your family had done the same."

Sally hesitated.

"What my family did to you… was wrong. But it's too late now, Miss McKendrick, we're all gone. Edward knew nothing. Taking him away from his home will not give you revenge."

There was a chilly silence. Then Miss McKendrick was heard again.

"As you say. It's too late."

Ellie heard a low, creaking sound.

Snap!

Ellie leapt back as the flat part of the next stair shot upwards, as though on a hinge. It caught her firmly across the legs.

Another stair lashed out at her. Then another.

"Hurry!" Sally squeezed Ellie's hand and led her down. "She's putting obstacles in our way. She must be afraid."

They fought their way downward. All the stairs were now snapping at them. Ellie stamped them down.

"Now!" Sally reached ground level a step ahead of Ellie. "The cellar! Quickly!"

Ellie gave a yell, as one of the white floor tiles dropped away beneath her. A black tile followed. The whole of the hall floor had become a kind of causeway that was crumbling piece by piece beneath their feet.

"Keep moving!" Sally was shouting. "We're almost there!"

Before them was the door to the cellar steps. Ellie reached for the handle.

She screamed as she found herself clutching the head of a hissing snake.

She heard Miss McKendrick's mocking laughter from beyond the door.

"Don't give in to her!" Sally grasped Ellie by the arms. "There's nothing there! She's simply playing on your fears."

Ellie concentrated hard.

The snake's head became a door handle again.

"Now!" Sally flung open the door. "Down!"

They ran down the steps.

They found themselves standing in darkness, illuminated only by a single beam of light right in the centre of the stone-walled chamber.

And in the lightbeam, standing immobile, was Edward.

"Edward!" Ellie ran forward, then stopped.

Edward's eyes stared wildly at her. But he gave no response.

"What's wrong with him?"

"He can hear us," Sally answered. "But not answer. She's using her power as a Spirit Guide. He's about to be judged."

"And you," said a voice, "have arrived just in time to hear the judgment."

They turned to see Miss McKendrick standing behind them. She was holding her cane, and had her book open and ready.

Ellie looked from one young woman to the other. In life, they must have been about the same age, yet Miss McKendrick now looked so much older than Sally – tired and drawn, with hurt in every line of her face.

"You may preach at me, Miss Sally," Miss McKendrick said. "But can you deny that Edward's trial is long overdue? No. His sins must now be judged."

She took a step towards Edward.

"And tonight, he comes with me to the place of all sinners."

She began to read from the book.

"Misuse of Spiritual Powers. Theft of Mortal Property…"

Ellie put her hands to her ears, as a hideous noise came from somewhere deep beneath the cellar. It was a mixture of all the worst sounds imaginable – screaming, and weeping, and moaning. She could hear the sound of someone falling downstairs… a young woman's horrified cry… Mingled in were sounds from other eras… swords connecting on the battlefield… and the distant roar of gunfire.

Miss McKendrick stood for a moment, absorbing it all, like someone basking in the sun. With every sound, she seemed to grow taller and stronger. Her voice became louder as she addressed Edward.

"Master Edward, as the final Fitzberranger you are the symbol of every sin committed by your family. And the victims are always those weaker than yourselves…"

With a yell of fury, she threw down the heavy book, sending it crashing to the stone floor.

She could no longer hide her pain. Tears were streaming down her cheeks. She screamed into Edward's face.

"You obnoxious child! I was unhappy for *three whole years* because of you! And your family abandoned me! They drove me *to my death*!"

Sally caught Ellie's eye. Her lips mouthed two words:

The brooch.

Ellie slipped it to her.

Sally swooped for the book and picked it up.

Miss McKendrick turned back. Her eyes gleamed. Her face was set.

"Very well," Sally said. The background noise faded a little. "My family had to atone for what it had done. And punishment has been served. Ellie explained to me. Our home is destroyed. But that must be all. Edward must still have a fair hearing."

She held out the brooch.

"And he can call several witnesses to support him."

She looked at the book.

"Others have seen Edward, throughout the decades. As recorded here. 1938… the youngest son of the Harvey family. 1954… a gardener. 1969…"

Ellie strained to hear. There were voices. A babble of distant speech.

She looked at the brooch. It was glowing.

"And those spirits…" Sally continued. "Are now coming back."

She held the brooch high.

"*Veritas vos liberabit!*"

Miss McKendrick leapt at Sally, knocking the brooch from her hand. But too late.

Around the cellar, figures were appearing. A boy in a 1930s suit and school cap. An elderly man dressed in gardening clothes. A long-haired young woman in a flowing dress and beads.

"All of them lived or worked or stayed at Inchwood," Sally continued. "All of them saw Edward in their lifetime. They saw what he did, the good things as well as the bad. And all of them are now his allies."

Miss McKendrick turned, as the group of ghostly figures closed in on her. There was a soldier from World War One. An elderly woman in a print dress. More children.

As she stared at the other spirits, Miss McKendrick's expression changed. The face of a different woman appeared – younger, more vulnerable. She looked at Edward, and then at Ellie, as though seeing them for the first time.

"They will now escort you, Miss McKendrick," Sally said. "They will escort you to your rest."

The figures closed in further. Their faces were not

threatening, but friendly. They reached out their hands in welcome to Miss McKendrick.

Ellie met Miss McKendrick's eye. For a moment, Ellie was transported back to the picnic where they had sat and laughed together.

Then Miss McKendrick disappeared into the centre of the crowd.

At the same moment, the lightbeam surrounding Edward vanished.

And the ground beneath their feet began to shake.

Sally made a grab for Edward's hand and pulled him over to her. With her other hand, she grabbed Ellie's arm.

"Run!"

Ellie paused just long enough to snatch up the brooch. Then she followed Sally.

They ran for the steps. The whole of the ghostly house was shaking and disintegrating. As they reached the hall, the walls and floor fell away around them. They found themselves flying into total darkness.

A light appeared, in the distance.

Sally clasped Ellie and Edward to her.

"Hold tight!"

Ellie found herself lying very still, in a silence interrupted only by the distant sound of water.

She opened her eyes. She was lying on the nursery floor, next to the rocking horse.

She sat up. Nearby, by the train set, lay Edward.

And standing over them was Sally.

Slowly, shakily, Ellie got to her feet.

"Sally." Edward rose and moved forward. "Well. Er… How awfully nice to see you again."

Sally embraced him.

"I say, steady on!" Edward squirmed. "Mortal watching."

He paused.

"Thank you. Both of you. Jolly grateful, and all that…"

He looked around.

"Has she gone now?"

"Yes," Sally answered. "At last, she can rest."

Ellie hesitated.

"In spite of what she did. I really hope she can."

"Now." Sally held out her hand, and the book reappeared. "Your trial is not finished, Edward. I think it's time you *did* receive judgment. From a more reliable Spirit Guide."

"Oh, Sally!" Edward whined. "Must I?"

"Until you receive judgment," Sally told him, "the barrier around you remains in force. You'll be trapped forever. Remember the family motto? The truth will set you free. As Miss McKendrick has just discovered."

She smiled, a little mischievously, as she read the book.

"Dear me, you *have* been a bad boy, haven't you? Stair carpets… pudding basins… motor car tyres…"

Edward stood like a prisoner in the dock.

"But what about the *other* pages?" Sally looked at

the opposite page, and at other left-hand pages. "The ones Miss McKendrick didn't mention? 1940. A small girl, just five years old, evacuated here from London, went a whole week without sleep. She was homesick, and cried from dusk 'til dawn. Then one night, she slept. And the next morning, she was happy. When asked why, she said: "The funny boy came and made me laugh. He told me a nice story, and did some magic. And then I was all right again.""

Edward smiled modestly.

"Well, anything but the waterworks."

"1963," Sally read another example, "in the wintertime. All the paths to the house mysteriously cleared themselves of snow. 1968, a cricket match played here was won for the village. Players on the other team said the ball seemed to take on a life of its own..."

Edward grinned.

"Well, they were a man short."

"Of course," Sally said. "I *am* your sister. And therefore, hardly the most impartial judge. What I really need, to make the decision a fair one, is some kind of independent witness, someone who can vouch for the fact that you've reformed. Someone... different from our kind. Maybe even someone from the mortal world itself?"

Ellie became aware that Sally was looking at her.

"Ellie," Sally said. "I see Edward behaved badly towards you to begin with. But..."

"Oh, that's all changed now!" Ellie rushed forward, then remembered her ankle, which was growing sorer by the minute. She winced. "Edward only went with

Miss McKendrick because of me. If it wasn't for him, I'd still be trapped in the priest's hole downstairs. I'd have drowned, probably! And he helped me get off the island, too. I'd say he's definitely reformed." She looked at Sally. "Well, as much as he's going to."

"Thank you, Ellie," Sally said. "Well, Edward. Weighing one side against the other, there is really only one judgment to which I can come. And that is –"

"Ellie!"

Ellie spun round. It was Charlie's voice.

She turned back.

Edward and Sally were nowhere to be seen.

She looked at the portrait across the room. Sally stood there again, motionless, a painted canvas.

"Ellie! Where are you?"

Ellie opened her hand. The brooch was still clutched there.

She hid it again quickly.

"I'm here!"

The door flew open.

"Where have you *been*?" Charlie demanded. "We've been looking everywhere for you! Have you seen what's going on down there? We almost drowned! Are you OK?"

He stared at Ellie.

"What are you wearing?"

For once, he wasn't acting. He looked genuinely worried. And his trouser-legs were wet.

Mum stood behind him, equally wet, her face strained and anxious.

"We couldn't get the door open! There was water pouring underneath! Mum and I have been standing on the kitchen table for the last hour! We've only just got out –"

He paused, and turned.

Marcus stood there, in a voluminous dressing-gown, yawning.

"What's going on?"

Chapter Seventeen

Ellie held out her paintbrush to the canvas, adding the last dab of black paint to the timbers of the Manor.

She sighed.

The painting was finished. Just like her stay at Inchwood.

Marcus had confirmed it to Mum a few days ago. The damage would take months, and require millions of pounds, to repair. There was no chance now of Inchwood opening to the public this summer – if ever.

Ellie had accompanied Mum and Marcus on a visit to Miss Harvey. For once, Marcus wasn't able to find much to say. Miss Harvey didn't seem angry, or upset, or even particularly surprised to hear the news. She listened to what they had to tell her. Then she went on planning the roster for the church flowers. Ellie quietly left the brooch for her on the mantelpiece.

There had been plenty of time for Ellie to finish her painting. Everyone was preparing to go. Their belongings – those that had survived the flood – were packed and ready to be loaded into the car. Thankfully, little of the water had reached the scullery, or any of Ellie's own things.

Ellie stepped out of the flat into the hall. Furniture had been ruined, chairs soaked, damp absorbed into the panelling. All around the tunnel entrances were piles of waste and mud. Some areas of the house were fenced off altogether, with red and white striped tape that said: DANGER. DO NOT PASS. Marcus had managed to round up one or two volunteers to assist with the clearing up, but it was an impossible task.

She walked up the staircase for the last time. On the lower stairs, the rich red carpet was wet and had turned to a darker shade.

She winced a little as she crossed the corridor. Her ankle still felt tender.

She entered the nursery slowly.

She was surprised to see Edward standing there, quite openly, not even bothering to hide. He was at the window, his back to her, staring out at the tops of the tall chestnut trees.

Ellie couldn't resist it. Very softly, she crept up on him.

"Boo!"

Edward took a violent leap. He spun round.

"What –? What are you doing?"

Ellie wasn't prepared for his reaction. He looked shocked… hurt. Almost ready to cry.

"Sorry… I thought…"

"Very funny," Edward said. He moved away quickly towards his damaged train set. "I ask you… Of all the things you could have landed on, you had to pick this."

"Well," Ellie said. "It helped us solve the mystery."

There was a long silence.

Eventually, Ellie said:

"So. Did you…"

Edward hesitated.

Then he smiled. He looked at the portrait of Sally on the wall.

"Yes. The judgment went my way. I'm free now." He looked down again at the toy engine. "Even though I've nowhere to go."

He blinked.

"Thanks for sticking up for me. I doubt it would have gone the way it did, without you."

There was another silence.

"I suppose you'll be leaving soon?"

"Yes," Ellie said. "Journeyback's pulling out. For now. They haven't quite given up, though. Marcus is determined this place will open one day. And there's loads of cleaning up to do. You'll still have some people to scare."

Edward brightened a little.

"Good."

He turned back to Ellie.

"Where do you go next?"

"Back to London," Ellie answered. "Journeyback want Mum to stay on. They've got a new project for her. A town house. It's only twenty minutes from home. And it's not far from where my Dad lives."

"I've got my wish, then," Edward said. "To be left alone. In my own house."

Ellie moved closer to him.

"You're free now. You're not trapped here any more. You could have gone with the other spirits… with Sally…"

"And to what?" Edward demanded. "What is there for me, away from here? No. This is where I belong."

He looked down at the remains of the signal box.

"Oh, don't worry about me. You still have your life… enjoy it. I'm just part of history."

He turned his gaze towards the bookshelves.

"I died a long time ago."

There was another silence.

"I want to come back," Ellie said. "Once they start the restoration. I'm sure I can find an excuse…"

The clock on the nursery mantelpiece struck the hour.

Reluctantly, Ellie moved away.

"I've got to go now, Edward. Mum wants us to set off straight after lunch."

She lingered for a moment.

"You know that trick you did, when you helped me get out of the priest's hole… You couldn't do it to all of you, could you? Just for a minute?"

Edward paused. Then he closed his eyes hard in concentration.

A moment later, his whole form became solid.

Ellie walked over and put her arms around him.

He felt so real…

"I say, steady on!" Edward put on a show of struggling. "Don't go all soppy on me! Just like a girl. Honestly, sometimes you're worse than Sally…"

He took a deep breath.

"Oh, crikey…"

He moved his arms to return the hug.

Ellie paused at the door.

"I'll make sure people don't forget you. I'd like to write something about you, send it to that website. People ought to know…"

Edward didn't look back at her. He moved to the piano and sat down.

He began to play, softly, clumsily, hitting the wrong note occasionally.

And as Ellie watched him, he began to fade.

For a moment, the keys continued to play themselves.

Then there was silence.

Ellie closed the nursery door.

In the corridor, she met Marcus. He had an expression much like that of Edward. But worse. He looked like a little boy who'd had all his toys taken away.

Ellie moved up to him.

"I'm sorry, Marcus."

"Onward and upward," Marcus said. "New horizons. New doors. They're giving me two new sites in London to manage."

He paused.

"Smaller ones. Including the one your Mum's going to. You won't have seen the last of me, just yet."

He shook his head.

"I won't be sorry to go. You think: countryside –

great! No worries there. Farmers' markets and flower shows. And what did I get? Priceless paintings being destroyed. Earthquakes. Floods…"

He moved away towards the Site Office.

Ellie stepped out of the front door onto the gravel path. She took a final look up at the house.

It had seemed so magical once. Those ancient walls.

Now, she knew what they had to hide.

She looked at the nursery window. But there was no one to be seen.

She moved over to their packed car. Charlie was already standing waiting, and his holdall was in the boot. Ellie had never seen anyone pack so fast.

He'd been almost nice, since the flood. Hadn't once called her "miniature one" or "small person".

"Hello, small person."

Ellie stopped walking.

There was a pause before she said: "Hello."

"Can't wait to be home." Charlie clambered into the car. "Seeing my mates this weekend. Pizza… go bowling… If I find out who's responsible for that flood, I'll kiss 'em."

Ellie hoped he wouldn't.

"Ellie!" Mum's voice said. "Haven't we forgotten something?"

She came struggling out of the house, carrying Ellie's easel – and the painting of the Manor.

"Oh, crikey!" Ellie moved to collect them. "I'm awfully sorry."

Mum frowned.

"*Awfully sorry... Crikey...?*"

Ellie hastily bundled the easel into the car.

"Can I put this on top?" She carried the painting round to the boot of the car just as Mum was about to close it. "I don't want it to get damaged. You never know. It might be worth something, one day. You might be selling copies of it here. I could make your fortune. Pay for the whole place to be repaired..."

The car door closed after her.

In the boot, within the painting, there was a flicker of movement.

Unseen by anyone in the car, a small, blond-haired figure in a tweed suit stepped out of the painted front door of the Manor, and walked into the foreground of the picture.

Edward waited there a moment, grinning, long enough to give the real house a little wave as the car moved away.

Then he stepped back into hiding within the frame.

The car zoomed off along the drive.

THE END

Ellie and Edward's adventures will continue in:

The Spirit of London

Enjoyed this? Why not read…

THE ALIEN IN THE GARAGE
AND OTHER STORIES
ROB KEELEY

Neil's little brother is driving him mad. There can't really be an alien living in the garage… can there?

Luke is bored. Adam has too much to do. Until they decide to swap lives…

A camping trip takes a spooky turn when a ghost story seems to be coming true…

These are just some of the tales in this funny and sometimes scary collection. You can also find out whether Liam and Justin would eat earwigs, why aliens like custard creams, and what exactly is the sinister creature lurking outside the tent…

The Alien in the Garage and Other Stories will appeal to boys and girls aged 8-12… And parents reading the stories to their children! Written for those with a boundless imagination, a strong sense of humour and a desire to learn more about their world.

Available now from Matador in paperback and eBook

Enjoyed this? Why not read…

THE (FAIRLY) MAGIC SHOW
AND OTHER STORIES
ROB KEELEY

Molly has just one day to become a magician...

**There's someone very special in Mrs Hoskins' class.
The question is – who?**

A skipping rope holds the power of time travel...

These are just some of the tales in this second collection
of funny, sometimes scary stories from Rob Keeley.

Available now from Matador in paperback and eBook

Enjoyed this? Why not read…

THE DINNER CLUB
AND OTHER STORIES
ROB KEELEY

Being on home dinners gives Aidan the chance to make some money…

A bridesmaid and a page chase a runaway wedding cake…

Mia and her Dad turn detective...

These are just some of the tales in Rob Keeley's new collection.

Available now from Matador in paperback